# A RELATIONSHIP OF SITUATIONSHIP

## A TANGLED MIND, A SILENT PEN: "PANDEY'S POETIC CONFLICT"

HRITIK YOGESH PANDEY

This book, A Relationship of Situationship, is dedicated to none but to myself.
And by this, I mean the I who stands lost in the echoes of a journey once begun
by two, only to be forsaken, left behind at a crossroad where the path
diverged—betrayed and abandoned, now wandering alone.

# Contents

# Contents

# Contents

# Contents

# Contents

# Preface

<u>When my Pen Starts Overthinking , It Starts Inking Emotions out.</u>

" " *Sometimes, when my words overthink,*
*I hear them whisper, sharp and distinct:*
*"Pandey, satisfy your soul first,*
*Forget the world, its loud and cursed." -*
*Pandey, Forget the shadow you painted so deep,*
*In corners of thought where memories sleep.*
*Yet, as the echoes start to fade,*
*Conflicts rise, and choices jade,*
*Release the ties to that imagined muse,*
*A vision that haunts, a ghost I choose...,*
*I sit amidst this warring tide,*
*Me—the castaway, set aside.*
*Neither my thoughts bend to my plea,*
*Nor my pen surrenders, wild and free.*

*Lost in a loop, I'm a voice unheard,*
*A poet silenced, a flightless bird.*
*And there I dwell, alone and torn,*
*Where stories end, and wounds are born.*
*But the storm within never relents,*
*Conflicts churn, my mind invents.*
*Each thought collides, a restless tide,*
*And I, the poet, pushed aside.*
*My pen falters; it won't obey,*
*Words, once vibrant, now decay.*
*I call to them, but they refuse,*
*Both muse and ink leave me confused.*
*I'm left stranded, my voice undone,*
*A prisoner where thoughts outrun.*
*Neglected, lost in my own design,*
*Where stories die, and shadows align.*
*Here I sit, within this fray,*
*A poet silenced, night and day.*
*For neither thought nor word will yield,*
*And so, my heart becomes my shield...!'*

*- Hritik .Y. Pandey*

" *In the quiet corners of his once-lively room, Pandey sits with a pen in hand and a blank page before him. Time seems suspended, the air heavy with memories and unresolved emotions. The same hands that once danced across the page, weaving shayris and lyrics from the whispers of his heart, now tremble with hesitation.*

*His mind, once a cascade of verses and melodies, feels choked with confusion, as though the strings of his creativity have been severed.*"

# Prologue

In a world where secrets are as common as the air we breathe, two lives entwine in the most unexpected of ways.

Pandey, a man with eyes that have witnessed both the beauty and darkness of life, carries an air of mystery that keeps even the closest of companions at bay. His past is a maze of shadows, a tale only whispered in corners, but his present is defined by purpose. His every move is calculated, every word chosen with precision, yet the burden of what he hides weighs heavier than any of the answers he could give.

On the other side, there is Vanya Jain—an enigma wrapped in a persona of quiet strength and unwavering resolve. Her life seems perfect from the outside: a successful career, a network of friends, and a family that adores her. But beneath the surface, Vanya struggles with a truth she's been avoiding, one that is poised to reveal itself in the most dramatic of fashions. Her intelligence is sharp, her ambition ruthless, but it is the unspoken things—the fears, the regrets—that threaten to break her.

Fate, as it often does, brings them together—two souls, each carrying their own burdens, crossing paths in a way neither could have anticipated. The first meeting was anything but ordinary. Vanya had been a challenge—one that Avi, a mutual acquaintance, had handed to Pandey. He had been tasked with breaking her walls, with drawing out the hidden truths buried deep inside her. At the time, they were nothing more than strangers, each unaware of the complex layers that lay beneath the surface.

Pandey had taken on the challenge with his usual cold determination, prepared to face the elusive woman with every calculated strategy he could muster. He was used to control, used to being the one pulling the strings. But Vanya was different. Her fierce independence, her defiance, and her own carefully constructed barriers made her a puzzle he had yet to solve.

And yet, as time wore on, their interactions shifted. What began as a mission to uncover secrets soon morphed into something more—a bond that neither had expected. The lines between professional and personal blurred, and the calculated dance of trust and resistance became a fragile thing they both struggled to navigate.

In the end, it was love that bloomed between them. It wasn't instantaneous, nor was it easy. They had fought against it, denied it, even feared it. But as they stood together, no longer strangers but partners in both challenge and triumph, they realized that what had once seemed like a battle of wills had transformed into a deep connection, an understanding born from the very things that had once divided them.

Their journey ahead would challenge everything they knew, forcing them to confront their darkest fears and deepest desires. The truths they sought were not always the answers they wanted, but in each other, they found the courage to face them. And as their story unfolds, they will discover that the only thing more dangerous than the darkness they hide is the light they've yet to embrace.

# CHAPTER ONE

# The First Crack

*It wasn't always this way. There was a time when words flowed from him effortlessly, like the rivers of his native hills. His partner, once his muse and confidant, had been a silent partner in his creations.*

*Her laughter lingered in the cadence of his rhymes, her warmth infused in the metaphors he crafted. But when she left—without reason, without closure—Pandey's words seemed to leave with her. The betrayal wasn't merely of love but of the trust that had been the foundation of his art.*

*The mystery of her departure haunts him. Each attempt to write brings her face to mind, not as a muse but as a ghostly presence.*

*Her absence whispers accusations he cannot decipher, and his pen, once his solace, now feels like a tool of self-inflicted wounds. The page stares back at him, unyielding, a stark reminder of the creativity he's lost.*

# The Wishpers of Ink

*In a quiet room, where voices fade,*
*Pandey found solace in lines he laid.*
*A pen his tongue, the paper his ear,*
*A silent exchange, both distant and near.*

*An introvert's world, too vast for speech,*
*In ink and curves, his heart could reach.*
*No crowd to judge, no gaze to meet,*
*Just thoughts flowing, steady, discreet.*

# A Symphony of Silence

*Words were his armor, sharp and true,*
*Stories unspoken, feelings askew.*
*Each line a thread, weaving his tale,*
*His triumphs, his losses, his joys frail.*

*He wrote not for fame, nor applause to greet,*
*But for the harmony his soul could meet.*
*The weight of the world, too heavy to bear,*
*Lightened through words, laid plain and bare.*

# She came, She stayed

*And then she came, a storm too bright,*
*Her laughter, a spark, her eyes, a light.*
*He wrote of her presence, her quiet charm,*
*A world he built to shield her from harm.*

*His pen danced for her, a rhythm divine,*
*His paper sang, "Forever, she's mine."*
*Yet in this joy, a shadow crept,*
*A theft unnoticed, as promises wept.*

# The Theft of his Soul

*For she stole his muse, his pen's refrain,*
*Left him adrift in a sea of pain.*
*His ink dried up, his thoughts askew,*
*A writer undone, with nothing to pursue.*

*Not a thief by hand, but one of the heart,*
*She severed his words, tore them apart.*
*His paper now blank, his pen now still,*
*A void she carved, he could not fill.*

# A Heart that speaks in Lines

*Pandey was not a man of verbal grace,*
*His silence misunderstood, a lonely embrace.*
*But his pen and paper, they spoke his mind,*
*A language unique, one of a kind.*

*Through sonnets and prose, he found his way,*
*To speak of nights and golden days.*
*An introvert's dialogue, tender, deep,*
*A connection forged where others couldn't leap.*

# Lost in Void

*But now, as he sat in that empty room,*
*The silence screamed, a deafening gloom.*
*His thoughts, once eager to find their place,*
*Wandered aimlessly, a lost embrace.*

*He held his pen, a friend grown cold,*
*Its weight now heavy, its story untold.*
*The paper stared, blank and white,*
*A mocking canvas, devoid of light.*

# A Bond Beyond Words

*For pen and paper were more than tools,*
*They were allies, they were schools.*
*Teaching him to feel, to dream, to heal,*
*To craft a world no one could steal.*

*But she, unknowingly, stole that bond,*
*Left him stranded, a writer forlorn.*
*Her memory lingered, a cruel refrain,*
*A muse turned thief, a source of pain.*

# The Echoes of Creation

*Still, deep within, a whisper stirred,*
*A faint reminder, a calling heard.*
*The ink is yours, the lines your song,*
*No theft can silence where you belong.*

*For even when words seem lost in haze,*
*The soul remembers its writing days.*
*The pen will move, the paper will hear,*
*The voice of Pandey, steadfast, clear.*

# A Writer Reclaimed

*And so he sits, in shadows deep,*
*A heart once broken, begins to leap.*
*With trembling hand, the pen does glide,*
*His voice returns, no longer denied.*

*He writes of pain, of loss, of love,*
*Of life below and stars above.*
*His story flows, unbridled, free, A tapestry of all he can be.*

# The Shadows of her Life

*In the stillness of nights, where silence reigns,*
*Pandey sits, his heart heavy with pains.*
*The pen trembles within his grasp,*
*The ink refusing its gentle clasp.*

*He tries to write, to weave her name,*
*But words elude him, shy and lame.*
*Vanya, the muse, the betrayal, the song,*
*A love once right, now eternally wrong.*

# Three Years of a Beautiful Lie

*For three long years, his world she held,*
*In her laughter, his chaos was quelled.*
*In her gaze, he found his home,*
*A sanctuary where his soul could roam.*

*He offered her love, pure and wide,*
*Like the ocean embracing the moonlit tide.*
*Each word he wrote, each song he sang,*
*Echoed her name, as his heartstrings rang.*

*Yet, in her silence, a shadow grew,*
*A storm Pandey neither saw nor knew.*
*The betrayal came, sharp and cold,*
*A story of love left untold.*

# The Day of the End

*The last time he saw her, the world stood still,*
*A moment etched, against his will.*
*Her eyes met his, a fleeting glance,*
*The final waltz of a broken romance.*

*She walked away, without a word,*
*Leaving echoes of love unheard.*
*Pandey stood, rooted in that space,*
*Forever caught in her vanishing trace.*

# The Haunting Grip of Time

*Though time has passed, it bears no balm,*
*His wounds remain, devoid of calm.*
*He lives in that moment, frozen in place,*
*A prisoner to her phantom embrace.*

*The streets they walked, the songs they hummed,*
*The promises made, now cold and numbed.*
*Each corner he turns, her shadow he sees,*
*A ghost that whispers through the breeze.*

# The Betrayal's Song

*Oh, how he tries to sing her name,*
*But his voice falters, wracked with shame.*
*The melodies crack, the lyrics fade,*
*A broken song, in memories laid.*

*He strums the guitar, its strings unkind,*
*Each note a dagger to his mind.*
*Her betrayal, a chord that won't relent,*
*A dissonance in love's lament.*

# Words That Won't be Written

*And so, Pandey turns to the page,*
*Seeking solace, a placc to assuage.*
*But the pen rebels, the ink retreats,*
*A blank canvas of incomplete beats.*

*He tries to write of love and pain,*
*Of sunshine lost in torrential rain.*
*Yet every line feels foreign, astray,*
*A reflection of a heart led away.*

# A Love That Lingers

*And so, Pandey turns to the page,*
*Seeking solace, a place to assuage.*
*But the pen rebels, the ink retreats,*
*A blank canvas of incomplete beats.*

*He tries to write of love and pain,*
*Of sunshine lost in torrential rain.*
*Yet every line feels foreign, astray,*
*A reflection of a heart led away.*

# The Conflicted Soul

*In anger, he curses her name aloud,*
*In love, he whispers it, soft and proud.*
*The duality tears his soul in two,*
*A battle of hearts, old and new.*

*He yearns to move, to leave her behind,*
*Yet the chains of memory forever bind.*
*Each step he takes, he looks around,*
*For traces of her, where none are found.*

# Reflections in the Void

*Pandey knows, deep within,*
*This is a war he cannot win.*
*For even in hate, love finds its way,*
*A stubborn ghost that's here to stay.*

*He questions himself, his worth, his plight,*
*How could he not see the fading light?*
*How could he not hear the lies she told,*
*The warmth that turned to distant cold?*

# A Hopeful Fuitility

*Yet in his brokenness, hope takes root,*
*A fragile flower, bearing no fruit.*
*He dreams of a day when he can write,*
*Of love renewed, of dawn's soft light.*

*He dreams of singing without the crack,*
*Of melodies pure, untainted, intact.*
*But the present mocks him, day by day,*
*A cruel reminder of love's decay.*

# Standing Still in the Last Goodbye

*Pandey remains, in that moment confined,*
*Where her eyes last met his, entwined.*
*The last time he held her, the last time he tried,*
*To keep her near, before she lied.*

*The world has moved, but not for him,*
*He lingers in shadows, cold and grim.*
*A boy, a man, a writer torn,*
*In love's ashes, forever worn.*

# A Silent Plea to the Universe

*If only the stars could answer his plea,*
*To unwrite the pain, to set him free.*
*If only his pen could find its way,*
*To write of tomorrow, not yesterday.*

*But for now, he stands in love's debris,*
*A poet lost, beneath memory's tree.*
*Vanya, his muse, his joy, his bane,*
*The sweetest love, the deepest pain.*

# The Eternal Echo

*And so, Pandey writes, though the words feel untrue,*
*IIis voice a whisper, his heart askew.*
*He knows one truth, amidst the strife,*
*Vanya will haunt him for all his life.*

*The ink may fade, the pages may tear,*
*But her shadow lingers, always there.*
*In the silence of nights, where love once shone,*
*Pandey writes, but never alone.*

# CHAPTER TWO

# The Arrival

*She stepped into a world brimming with chaos,*
*A kaleidoscope of colors, both bright and ferocious.*
*Her presence, a whisper, serene, and elusive,*
*A breeze that lingered, quiet yet intrusive.*
*From the hills of Shimla, where whispers grow loud,*
*To Delhi's hum beneath the urban shroud.*
*Vanya arrived, a silhouette framed in grace,*
*With walls so high, none could find their place.*
*Her laughter was rare, like a fleeting tune,*
*Her heartstrings tuned to a solitary moon.*
*A girl of silence, wrapped in distant light,*
*An enigma to the bold, a shadow in sight.*
*Her eyes, deep pools, held stories untold,*
*Of icy peaks and mornings gold.*
*Mountains and snow whispered through her gaze,*
*Yet no path for the curious her soul could blaze.*
*She carried the quiet of Shimla's hills,*
*Yet her silence spoke louder than Delhi's thrills.*
*And then there was Hritik, a name that roared,*
*Through college halls, his legend soared.*
*A charmer, a storm, his laughter rang clear,*
*His presence a beacon, drawing all near.*
*With charm as his sword, he bridged every chasm,*
*Yet in her, he found not awe, but a quiet phantasm.*

*She was the stillness to his reckless fire,*
*An echo of something that stirred deep desire.*
*While others were dazzled by his effortless might,*
*She stood apart, veiled in her quiet light.*
*To him, she was not just a girl in the crowd,*
*But a mystery wrapped in the gentlest shroud.*
*What stories lay behind her guarded stance?*
*What secrets hid in her faraway glance?*
*To Vanya, the world was a noise to endure,*
*But to Hritik, she was a puzzle too pure.*
*And so began the clash of stillness and storm,*
*Two lives intersecting, against the norm.*
*In a world brimming with chaos, their tale unfurled,*
*A collision of whispers and shouts in a restless world.*

# CHAPTER THREE

# Breaking the Ice

*"Can you melt her?" they jested, their challenge sharp,*
*A gauntlet thrown to Hritik, the campus spark.*
*With a grin that held both mischief and charm,*
*He took up the task, unshaken, disarmed.*
*And so began his journey, his unstruck harp,*
*To play for a heart so guarded and stark.*
*His overtures were gentle, a soft refrain,*
*A melody of patience in a world so vain.*
*A glance here, a gesture there,*
*A subtle dance, a delicate care.*
*He held a door; she walked through,*
*Not a word was spoken, but something felt new.*
*He offered notes, his heart a quiet plea,*
*She gave a view, a fleeting mystery.*
*Days turned to weeks, and their paths aligned,*
*Moments shared, though her thoughts confined.*
*A word exchanged, a silence broken,*
*A smile glimpsed, a bond unspoken.*
*She was the mountain, steadfast and still,*
*He was the river, flowing by will.*
*Until one night, beneath the celestial glow,*
*The stars bore witness to a tale in flow.*
*Four hours unbroken, their voices entwined,*
*In the quiet of the night, their hearts aligned.*
*He spoke of his journey, his triumphs, his plight,*

*Of cooking "**Akki Roti**" in the pale moonlight.*
*His words wove laughter, a balm to her guard,*
*And for the first time, her silence unbarred.*
*Her laughter rang, soft as a chime,*
*Echoing through the stillness of time.*
*He saw the sparkle that her silence concealed,*
*A glimpse of the warmth her walls had sealed.*
*Each story he shared, each jest he wove,*
*Carved a path to her heart, a treasure trove.*
*Her replies were soft, but her eyes held more,*
*A world opening slowly, a heart to explore.*
*And as dawn approached, painting skies anew,*
*Something had shifted, tender and true.*
*In the quiet of the night, a bridge was built,*
*Between her guarded world and his endless lilt.*
*"Can you melt her?" they had jested and laughed,*
*But it wasn't fire or force, just a gentle craft.*
*A note of patience, a song of care,*
*He didn't melt her, but met her there.*

# CHAPTER FOUR

# Shadows and Cigarette Trails

*Amidst the chaos of SAARC's grind,*
*Files shuffled, and deadlines timed.*
*Pandey and Vanya, two threads entwined,*
*Close in their orbit, yet blind by design.*
*A stage of competition, the world at play,*
*Legal minds sparring through night and day.*
*But behind the debates and moot court runs,*
*Brewing was a story not yet begun.*
*Avi and Pandey, a cigarette in hand,*
*Stepped out to breathe where the streetlights stand.*
*The smoke curled, the air turned thin,*
*Unaware of the storm that brewed within.*
*Pandey's gaze, sharp and unkind,*
*Caught a corner scene that froze his mind.*
*There sat Vanya, too close, too near,*
*To a man unknown, a specter unclear.*
*Her head dipped low as she caught his stare,*
*A shield of shame in the evening air.*
*But her guilt lit a fire in Pandey's chest,*
*A restless ache, a heart distressed.*
*"Why does it sting? What is this fire?"*
*He questioned the pain, the unspoken desire.*
*They were friends, just friends, he'd swear,*

Yet something was born in that silent glare.
The old man, a figure from her past,
Dug up emotions that Pandey thought would last.
He felt the pull, the crackling thread,
A story unspoken, a love misread.
Vanya sat still, her mind ablaze,
Lost in the web of guilt and haze.
She knew not why, but Pandey's glance,
Burned through her like a devil's dance.
The night stretched long, the stars bore witness,
To Pandey's silence, his quiet bitterness.
He drove away, the wheel his anchor,
But the scene replayed, a maddening clamor.
His heart ached, a storm untamed,
Yet no one was at fault, no one to blame.
Vanya's face lingered, her downcast eyes,
A thousand questions, no answers supplied.
Two days passed, the air grew thick,
The moments between them, awkward and quick.
Pandey stood distant, his words refrained,
Yet Vanya felt a pull, her heart restrained.
Their talks resumed in a fragile way,
The ghost of that evening kept at bay.
But the unspoken truth in their posture lay,
In glances stolen, emotions betrayed.
"Why did it matter? Why did it sting?"
Vanya thought, as her soul took wing.
Pandey's silence was a blade too sharp,
Etching guilt into her fragile heart.
When they finally spoke, the words were few,
Yet in their tone, the storm broke through.
Close, too close, their voices low,
A magnetic pull they couldn't outgrow.
The body betrayed what the mind denied,
Hands too near, hearts open wide.

Yet the label stayed—a "friendship" framed,
While the fire beneath burned untamed.
The story unfolds in shadows and light,
In awkward days and sleepless nights.
Pandey and Vanya, two souls in a dance,
Bound by a love that hid in a glance.
Every moment between them was layered with doubt,
Words unsaid, fears never spoken out.
They circled each other, like moths to a flame,
Afraid of the fire, yet drawn just the same.
Their days were filled with mundane routines,
Papers to file, emails, and screens.
But beneath the veneer of their work and talk,
Lingered an energy too wild to mock.
Vanya's laugh would ripple through the air,
A sound so vivid, it laid Pandey bare.
He'd steal a glance, caught in her glow,
Feeling things he could never show.
And Vanya, bold but secretly shy,
Saw something in Pandey she couldn't deny.
In his quiet demeanor, his patient ways,
She found a calm amidst her chaotic days.
But there was a tension that neither addressed,
A longing too raw to leave unexpressed.
Their connection was fragile, a porcelain thread,
Caught between the living and the undead.
Every laugh, every glance, every fleeting touch,
Spoke of a bond that felt too much.
Yet they held back, afraid of the fall,
Trapped in a maze, in love's enthrall.
They were close, yet a chasm apart,
Two halves of a whole, Two threads of the same fabric, torn yet
yearning to entwine anew.
And as the days wore on, their silence grew loud,
An unspoken symphony, a gathering cloud.

*In this undefined space, they lingered still,*
*A bond unbroken, yet unfulfilled.*
*And as the story unfolded, the truth remained,*
*That in each other's eyes, their souls were chained.*

# CHAPTER FIVE

# The Unseen Beginning

*In the labyrinth of fleeting days and unspoken intent,*
*Pandey and Vanya began their descent.*
*Not into chaos, not into despair,*
*But into something fragile, delicate, and rare.*
*Without a sign, a hint, or a clue,*
*Two souls unaware, slowly drew.*
*Their paths crossed not with sparks or fire,*
*But with quiet moments, shaped by desire.*
*He, a shadow in his own tale,*
*Shy, reserved, behind an introvert's veil.*
*His voice was soft, his words were few,*
*Yet in his silence, a world broke through.*
*She, on the other hand, was wild and free,*
*A tempest untamed, like waves in the sea.*
*Her laughter loud, her steps bold,*
*Her heart a furnace, her spirit untold.*
*Where he faded into corners, content to observe,*
*She claimed the room, all passion and verve.*
*To others, she was a blazing flame,*
*Her fierce opinions earning both scorn and acclaim.*
*Where gentler souls might inspire tender grace,*
*Her fiery temper occupied that space.*
*Her disdain, her boldness, her fearless refrain,*
*Were the echoes of home, of love's terrain.*
*A place where affection and fury entwined,*

*A tempestuous bond of hearts and minds.*
*Pandey watched from afar, his gaze unsure,*
*Drawn to the fire but fearing the lure.*
*He admired her strength, her unapologetic flair,*
*But doubted if he could ever stand there.*
*What could a shadow offer to a storm?*
*What warmth could a quiet soul transform?*
*Yet, life has its way of bridging divides,*
*Of entwining paths where opposites reside.*
*In small, unguarded moments they met,*
*Through shared silences they could not forget.*
*A late-night library, a coffee shop's hum,*
*In places mundane, the magic would come.*
*She caught him once, lost in thought,*
*Her fiery eyes softened by what she sought.*
*"Pandey," she teased, her voice a spark,*
*"Always in the shadows, afraid of the dark?"*
*He blushed, his words stumbled and fell,*
*Yet in his shy smile, a story did dwell.*
*And though she was wild, and he was restrained,*
*Something between them gently remained.*
*Her fire did not scorch; his shadow did not fade,*
*Instead, they danced in the balance they made.*
*For the flame needs the night to glow its brightest hue,*
*And the shadow finds solace in a fire's view.*
*In the labyrinth of fleeting days and unspoken intent,*
*Pandey and Vanya began their descent.*
*Not into chaos, nor into despair,*
*But into a connection, tender and rare.*

# CHAPTER SIX

# The Subtle Spark

*Mornings intertwined as college called,*
*Together they walked, the world enthralled.*
*Each sunrise brought their paths to meet,*
*In shared routines, their story found its beat.*
*His car awaited, parked by the lane,*
*A quiet chariot through chaos and strain.*
*Through Delhi's bustle, through honks and roars,*
*They traveled together, past the city's stores.*
*Her window framed the world in motion,*
*But inside the car, it was pure emotion.*
*Their silence spoke volumes, a curious thing,*
*A rhythm of comfort that words could not bring.*
*He stole glances when he thought she wouldn't see,*
*And she, in her stillness, let her guard roam free.*
*The streets blurred by, a cacophony of dreams,*
*Yet their quiet moments eclipsed the streams.*
*Dating was a word they dared not use,*
*Their hearts beat wild, yet they stood confused.*
*What name could encompass this fragile dance?*
*A connection of depth, born out of chance.*
*Was it love, that electric, aching fire?*
*Or merely a bond shaped by mutual desire?*
*Friends, perhaps, yet something more,*
*A situationship knocking at their core.*
*They shared playlists, swapped subtle grins,*

*A tangle of hearts where it all begins.*
*Her laughter lingered when he fumbled his jokes,*
*And his eyes softened when her confidence broke.*
*Lunches in the canteen stretched longer each day,*
*With conversations that meandered and swayed.*
*Books and coffee, inside jokes shared,*
*Moments of vulnerability, both unprepared.*
*She teased him endlessly about his quiet ways,*
*While he admired her boldness, her fearless gaze.*
*And yet, beneath the laughter, questions grew,*
*Unspoken doubts that neither could pursue.*
*Were they two friends, bound by time and fate,*
*Or something deeper, waiting at the gate?*
*Each glance they exchanged, each lingering pause,*
*Whispered a truth they could not cause.*
*At times, their closeness felt like a dream,*
*A fragile bubble afloat on life's stream.*
*But in the car, amidst the city's roar,*
*They found a stillness that was hard to ignore.*
*Her fingers brushing the edge of the seat,*
*His hand on the wheel, steady yet discreet.*
*A love undefined, or a bond in disguise?*
*The world saw nothing, but they saw it in their eyes.*
*A situationship, a phase unnamed,*
*A wild, uncharted path they claimed.*
*And so, they journeyed, together yet apart,*
*Navigating the maze of an uncertain heart.*

# The Surprise Visit

*One day, from campus, Vanya slipped away,*
*To Pandey's haven, mid-college day.*
*The lectures droned on, the world unaware,*
*While she walked a path few others would dare.*
*Pandey, unwell, lay cocooned in his bed,*
*A dull ache throbbing through his weary head.*
*Books and blankets cluttered the space,*
*A quiet retreat, his secret place.*
*But the solitude broke with the buzz of her call,*
*A spark in his gloom, a beacon to all.*
*"Open the door," her voice gently chimed,*
*Her presence, unexpected, yet perfectly timed.*
*He shuffled to greet her, groggy and pale,*
*Surprised by the sight of her, strong and hale.*
*With food in hand and care in her tone,*
*She bridged the gap he thought was his own.*
*Her arrival felt like a whirlwind's grace,*
*Transforming the energy within the space.*
*The lone boy's room, a bachelor's den,*
*Was soon set upon by hurried men.*
*Roommates scrambled, cleaning with haste,*
*Clearing the clutter, erasing the waste.*
*A clean kitchen, a welcome smile,*
*Her presence stayed, more than just a while.*

*She moved through the room with effortless ease,*
*A force of nature, as light as the breeze.*
*Folding blankets, stacking books high,*
*Bringing order to chaos under his shy eye.*
*"You live like this?" she teased with a grin,*
*As laughter filled spaces once quiet within.*
*She placed the food on his bedside table,*
*A small, simple meal, but nourishing, stable.*
*"Eat this," she said, her voice firm yet kind,*
*And in her tone, he found peace of mind.*
*For a boy used to loneliness, she was a light,*
*An anchor of warmth in his solitary night.*
*As he ate, they talked, their walls unwound,*
*Their voices merging, a harmonious sound.*
*Her laughter danced through the dim-lit room,*
*Chasing away the lingering gloom.*
*The stories they shared, the moments they spun,*
*Felt like a journey that had just begun.*
*The air grew thin with emotions untold,*
*A quiet intensity, fragile yet bold.*
*The walls bore witness, silent and still,*
*To something awakening, beyond their will.*
*Not love, not yet, but the seeds were sown,*
*In the quiet moments they now called their own.*
*When she left that day, the room felt vast,*
*A space now echoing with memories cast.*
*And Pandey lay there, his heart aglow,*
*A feeling stirring, a warmth to know.*

# The First Kiss

*A moment stolen, a glance too long,*
*A pause that silenced life's loudest song.*
*Eyes locked in a language unspoken,*
*Walls crumbled, their defenses broken.*
*Her touch, a whisper; his breath, a plea,*
*A spark ignited, wild and free.*
*The world outside faded away,*
*Time stood still as night claimed day.*
*The hum of the city, the ticking clock,*
*All drowned beneath their hearts' unlock.*
*Clothes undone, barriers shed,*
*A path untrodden, fearlessly tread.*
*Fingers traced stories along bare skin,*
*Each touch a revelation, a world within.*
*Her warmth met his, a blazing storm,*
*Their bodies entwined, perfectly formed.*
*Breath mingled in rhythms divine,*
*A symphony played beyond the confines of time.*
*The air was chilled, but the room was warm,*
*Their passion surged, defying the norm.*
*His lips sought hers, a tender ache,*
*Each kiss a promise they dared to make.*
*She held him close, a quiet command,*
*As waves of emotion slipped through their hands.*

*For hours they danced, a sacred rite,*
*Bodies and souls bathed in moonlight.*
*Every curve explored, every sigh was known,*
*A connection deeper than words could be shown.*
*Her hair spilled like silk, his hands a map,*
*Tracing a bond no force could unwrap.*
*The moon bore witness to their sacred flight,*
*Illuminating shadows with gentle light.*
*Each gasp, each cry, each tender sound,*
*Wove a tapestry where their hearts were bound.*
*A love undefined, raw and real,*
*A space where two hearts could fully feel.*
*As dawn crept in with its golden hue,*
*Their passion calmed, but their bond felt new.*
*Entwined in silence, they lay at rest,*
*Each heartbeat echoing the other's chest.*
*No words were spoken, for none could convey,*
*What their souls had shared in the night's display.*

# CHAPTER NINE

# Rituals of Love

*Vanya, wild as the sea at dawn,*
*Was everything Pandey had leaned upon.*
*Her spirit, untamed, a force of its own,*
*In her presence, his solitude was overthrown.*
*Sensual, seductive, unbound by fear,*
*She turned their love into a sphere so near.*
*A constant presence, vibrant and true,*
*A storm he welcomed, a world anew.*
*She moved through life with fearless grace,*
*A rebel heart in every space.*
*Her boldness was fire, unapologetic and raw,*
*A spark in the mundane, the wild he saw.*
*Pandey, the calm to her blazing storm,*
*Found in her chaos a comforted norm.*
*Where he was quiet, reflective, reserved,*
*She was the flame his spirit deserved.*
*Her laughter rang like a daring song,*
*A melody to which his heart belonged.*
*Each glance she cast, each word she said,*
*Painted colors where silence had spread.*
*She drew him out from his guarded stance,*
*Into a world of daring romance.*
*Their love was not quiet, nor was it loud,*
*It danced between storms and a soft shroud.*
*Each day brought a rhythm, a ritual of sorts,*

*Moments that wove through life's winding ports.*
*Mornings of whispers, nights full of heat,*
*A cadence of love neither could defeat.*
*Her touch ignited his skin with fire,*
*Every gesture fed an unending desire.*
*She met his calm with passion untamed,*
*Each moment together left neither the same.*
*Her wildness did not overpower his grace,*
*Together they carved a sacred space.*
*In stolen hours, their souls entwined,*
*A bond so fierce, a love unconfined.*
*Her daring merged with his quiet plea,*
*Their love became a tempest at sea.*
*Each meeting, a ritual—a burning fire,*
*Both consumed by the other's desire.*
*She taught him to live beyond the lines,*
*To savor chaos, to taste the divine.*
*And in her, he found a mirror so clear,*
*Reflecting the courage he had yet to endear.*
*Together, they defied the world's refrain,*
*Creating their own, unbroken chain.*
*They were opposites, yet seamlessly one,*
*Their love, a dance under moon and sun.*
*Vanya, wild as the sea at dawn,*
*Had become the light Pandey leaned upon.*

# CHAPTER TEN

# Aromatic Memories

*Their love carried scents of stolen days,*
*Of whispered moments and shadowed ways.*
*In dusty classrooms and fleeting halls,*
*It lingered softly, like rain that falls.*
*Her perfume trailed like a haunting spell,*
*A trace of jasmine and stories to tell.*
*His soap's embrace, clean and true,*
*A grounding presence that she always knew.*
*Together, they created an aromatic dance,*
*A timeless rhythm, a fragrant romance.*
*The smell of old books, ink on their hands,*
*Coffee's warmth from their favorite stands.*
*The faint musk of sweat after hurried walks,*
*Blended with memories born of deep talks.*
*Her laughter echoed, light as air,*
*Breaking his silences with tender care.*
*While his quiet presence, steady and strong,*
*Anchored her storms, a place to belong.*
*In their union, the universe rang,*
*A symphony of love, wild and unplanned.*
*Every touch was a word, tender and sweet,*
*Every glance a phrase, where souls would meet.*
*Their fingertips brushed, a fleeting caress,*
*Each spark igniting a shared confess.*
*The language they spoke had no need for sound,*

*In longing and haze, their hearts were bound.*
*They carried the scent of secrets and dreams,*
*Of moonlit nights and sunlit streams.*
*The world around them faded away,*
*Leaving only their love to light the way.*
*Her scent lingered on his shirt's soft sleeve,*
*A memory woven for him to retrieve.*
*His essence stayed on her skin, a trace,*
*A reminder of him in her sacred space.*
*Their love was a tapestry, stitched by the air,*
*With threads of passion, tenderness, and care.*
*Every stolen moment, every quiet embrace,*
*Etched eternity into their fleeting days.*
*They left a trail, invisible yet true,*
*A story told through scents only they knew.*

# CHAPTER ELEVEN

# A Drive Between Reality and Reverie

*The sun kissed the earth with its golden rays,*
*Painting the morning in soft, luminous haze.*
*Yet a cold breeze whispered in clandestine ways,*
*A quiet reminder of fleeting days.*
*It wasn't a holiday, nor a grand affair,*
*Yet joy danced lightly, lingering in the air.*
*For Pandey's heart hummed a secret refrain,*
*Knowing Vanya would soon ease his refrain.*
*He reached her hostel, his car softly purring,*
*A steady rhythm, emotions quietly stirring.*
*The streets were hushed, the world half-asleep,*
*Yet within him, a feeling began to seep.*
*Anticipation mingled with the dawn's first light,*
*As he waited for her, his anchor, his flight.*
*She emerged with grace, her steps a song,*
*Carrying more than charm as she moved along.*
*In her hand, a small pack of food she bore,*
*A simple gesture, yet it promised much more.*
*"You've not eaten, I just know you too well,"*
*Her words cast a spell where his emotions dwell.*
*A blend of care, love, and knowing intent,*
*In her presence, his worries were spent.*

*Her hair caught the sun, a cascade of flame,*
*And he marveled silently at the girl who came.*
*Not just as a friend or a passing face,*
*But as someone who gave his life a new grace.*
*She slid into the car, her warmth filling the space,*
*Her smile a light that time couldn't erase.*
*The wheel in his hands, yet his gaze softly stole,*
*Moments from her eyes, an unspoken console.*
*Her laughter was low, her words teasing and kind,*
*Each one a thread, their hearts intertwined.*
*She placed the food between them, a gentle command,*
*And without protest, he followed her plan.*
*As they drove through streets bathed in early gold,*
*Their connection grew, both quiet and bold.*
*The silence between them was not empty air,*
*But a language they spoke, intimate and rare.*
*She leaned back, her head tilted in ease,*
*While he glanced her way, his heart ready to seize.*
*In that moment, the world seemed to shrink,*
*To the hum of the engine, the coffee's faint ink.*
*Her presence, a balm, her care like a flame,*
*Burning quietly, without need of acclaim.*
*And as the sun climbed higher, dispelling the chill,*
*Pandey knew she was more than a fleeting thrill.*

# CHAPTER TWELVE

# The Hint of Rebellion

*As the roads unfolded like ribbons of fate,*
*The morning light danced, its glow innate.*
*Vanya turned, her eyes alight with play,*
*A spark igniting the dullness of day.*
*With a teasing smile, her voice feather-light,*
*She whispered a challenge, bold and bright:*
*"Why wait? Let's bunk the classes, escape the mundane,*
*Chase something unknown, break from the chain."*
*Pandey hesitated, his reason stood tall,*
*His logic a fortress, a cautionary wall.*
*"You're impossible," he muttered, half in jest,*
*Yet her laughter broke through, a joyous test.*
*It rippled like water, warm and free,*
*A melody daring him to let things be.*
*Her mischief was infectious, her spirit unbound,*
*And in her presence, no restraint could be found.*
*His lips curved upward, a reluctant grin,*
*Her wildness tugging at the calm within.*
*"Alright," he sighed, his resolve undone,*
*And with that decision, their journey begun.*
*The car sped forward, its engine a roar,*
*Leaving behind the city, its endless chore.*
*Onto the expressway, the world turned a blur,*
*A tapestry of motion created by her.*
*The hum of the tires, the wind's steady song,*

*Spoke of freedom, where they belonged.*
*Songs filled the car, a playlist shared,*
*Each lyric a story of moments they dared.*
*Their voices entwined in carefree refrain,*
*Weaving a harmony untainted by pain.*
*She drummed on the dashboard, a rhythmic beat,*
*While he stole glances, his heart skipping heat.*
*The road stretched ahead, vast and unknown,*
*A canvas for dreams they had not yet sown.*
*Fields blurred past in shades of green,*
*The world a backdrop to what lay between.*
*Her hair danced wildly, caught in the breeze,*
*A portrait of joy, unrestrained, at ease.*
*"Where to?" he asked, a laugh in his tone,*
*Her eyes sparkled as if she'd always known.*
*"Anywhere," she said, her voice a delight,*
*"As long as we're together, it feels just right."*
*And so, the road became their chosen escape,*
*A journey of freedom, love taking shape.*
*With every mile, their hearts grew closer,*
*Each moment richer, their connection bolder.*
*The rules of the world faded from view,*
*Leaving only the truth that they both knew.*
*It wasn't the destination that mattered most,*
*But the joy of being, their spirits engrossed.*

# CHAPTER THIRTEEN

# Of Headaches and Tender Care

*But joy took a pause as Vanya reclined,*
*Her head heavy, her spirit confined.*
*The laughter she wore now dimmed by the ache,*
*Her energy waning, as though a storm did break.*
*Pandey's eyes flickered with concern, a quiet plea,*
*Watching her shift, seeking some relief, some ease.*
*His heart stirred with an urge to protect,*
*To soothe the discomfort, to redirect.*
*Without a word, his hands gripped the wheel,*
*His thoughts quickened, a need to heal.*
*In a blink, he steered them to a small roadside stall,*
*The aroma of food beckoning, the call.*
*A humble joint, simple and true,*
*But in that moment, it was all they knew.*
*He parked the car, his gaze never leaving,*
*Her fragile form, her pain still cleaving.*
*"Stay here," he murmured, a gentle command,*
*As he hurried to fetch what he thought would withstand.*
*A tray of chai, steaming and sweet,*
*Pakodas crisp, golden, a savory treat.*
*The rain had begun to whisper its song,*
*A soft patter, rhythmic and strong.*
*It fell in delicate waves, tracing the glass,*

*As the world outside slipped quietly past.*
*He returned to the car, his hands full and warm,*
*Carrying comfort to shield her from harm.*
*With a tender smile, he handed her the cup,*
*"Here, drink this. It'll lift you up."*
*She took it gratefully, her fingers light,*
*The warmth of the chai a soft, gentle bite.*
*The pakodas, crisp and flaky, met her lips,*
*A simple gesture that warmed her fingertips.*
*Raindrops flirted with the car's cool frame,*
*Dancing in rhythm with a quiet flame.*
*The windshield fogged, the air thick with desire,*
*As romance whispered, its soft voice higher.*
*The world outside blurred in the rain's embrace,*
*But inside the car, there was only her face.*
*Their shared space felt sacred, untouched by time,*
*The moments fleeting, but infinitely sublime.*
*The steam rose gently, like a lover's sigh,*
*As the rain fell softly, the night drawing nigh.*
*In that stillness, something stirred, not loud but deep,*
*A connection forged while they both drifted to sleep.*
*As the food was consumed, and the tea was done,*
*Pandey's hand brushed hers, a touch just begun.*
*In that quiet act, a promise was made,*
*That no storm would break what together they'd laid.*
*And though her headache lingered, muted but near,*
*It was the warmth of his care that made it disappear.*

# The Roads of Longing

*With her spirit renewed, the drive resumed,*
*The car hummed softly, its engine gently groomed.*
*The skies above wore a gray, heavy veil,*
*As though the world itself had sighed, pale.*
*Clouds gathered like a blanket of sorrow,*
*Whispers of gloom falling on the morrow.*
*Yet their hearts, entwined in an unspoken grace,*
*Defied the melancholy, finding their place.*
*Though the world outside seemed caught in the gray,*
*Inside the car, their joy still held sway.*
*Her laughter had softened, but her smile remained,*
*The fleeting sadness by warmth was tamed.*
*They drove through the endless stretch of road,*
*A journey shared, a love in code.*
*The countryside blurred, a misty refrain,*
*But in that car, they were free from the strain.*
*As Agra neared, she leaned back with a sigh,*
*Her voice soft, yet laden with a quiet goodbye.*
*"Let's turn back, Pandey, there's work to comply,"*
*Her words a pull, like the earth to the sky.*
*A shadow flickered in the depths of her gaze,*
*As though the weight of duty was calling, a maze.*
*But even as she spoke, a part of her knew,*
*The journey they'd taken was something too true.*

*He nodded without question, a silent reply,*
*His heart twisting, though he didn't ask why.*
*Every moment with her, a treasure too rare,*
*A feeling of belonging, of being laid bare.*
*The thought of parting, even for a while,*
*Brought a heaviness that stole his smile.*
*Yet he understood, as all lovers must,*
*That moments like these were built on trust.*
*"Of course," he said, his voice soft, restrained,*
*Though his heart ached, in silence it pained.*
*For every second spent by her side,*
*Was a gift he cherished, an unspoken pride.*
*He turned the wheel, the road slipping by,*
*As Agra's distant skyline waved goodbye.*
*The car's hum now held a tender lull,*
*The space between them still beautifully full.*
*Though the journey back was not what they had planned,*
*There was no regret, no bitter reprimand.*
*For in each other's company, they had found,*
*A love that blossomed without bounds.*
*The gray skies above could weave their tale,*
*But their hearts, together, would always prevail.*
*And though the world outside might seem to frown,*
*Within their world, they could never be down.*

# CHAPTER FIFTEEN

# The Unexpected Exchange

*On the way back, a brief stop ensued,*
*Nature's call summoned, breaking their subdued.*
*The rain returned, now heavier, bold,*
*And in its embrace, a story untold.*
*As the car cruised at a reckless speed,*
*Passion overtook them, their desires freed.*
*Pandey's hands left the wheel, drawn to her curve,*
*A daring symphony of love and nerve.*
*Her lips sought his in a tender clash,*
*A kiss that ignited—a smoldering flash.*
*Their bodies drew closer, their breaths intertwined,*
*Fingers tracing secrets, unspoken, undefined.*
*The heat between them defied the rain's chill,*
*Moist skin meeting skin, igniting the thrill.*
*Her white kurta slipped, now a forgotten trace,*
*His blue shirt adorned her, a borrowed embrace.*
*The car surged forward at a hundred and ten,*
*Yet their focus was elsewhere, far beyond then.*
*Kisses deepened, their bodies aligned,*
*Cuddled in rhythm, passion enshrined.*
*Droplets of rain on the windows streamed,*
*Mirroring the heat in which their bodies gleamed.*
*The car was alive, not just from the speed,*
*But from the flame of their mutual need.*

*As his fingers traced the mark on her side,*
*A birthmark that made her impossible to hide,*
*He pulled her closer, her waist now his muse,*
*A captivating canvas he couldn't refuse.*
*The air was electric, the moment surreal,*
*A tempest of passion neither could conceal.*
*Though the car raced onward, their world stood still,*
*Bound by the pull of an irresistible will.*

# The Mark of Fascination

*In the stillness of passion, as their bodies met,*
*Pandey's wandering gaze found a secret inset.*
*A birthmark on her waist, dark and profound,*
*A treasure hidden, now gloriously found.*
*It wasn't just skin, it was poetry alive,*
*A symbol of allure, where his thoughts could dive.*
*The mark wasn't blemish, but a muse to ignite,*
*A focal point of wonder under the moon's pale light.*
*His fingers traced it with a reverent care,*
*Drawing invisible lines in the warm evening air.*
*Vanya shivered, not from cold but his touch,*
*A reaction so vivid, intimate, and such.*
*Her laughter softened, her breathing slowed,*
*As his hand lingered, its movements bestowed.*
*Exploring the curves he had yet to chart,*
*Each one a discovery, an echo in his heart.*
*The mark on her waist became his guide,*
*An emblem of closeness that refused to hide.*
*Pandey's lips followed where his fingers led,*
*His heart entwined with each word unsaid.*
*Vanya, caught between bashful and bold,*
*Let him explore the stories her body told.*
*Her shoulders a canvas, her collarbone art,*
*Every inch a rhythm that captured his heart.*

*She arched as his touch grew more sure,*
*Finding paths unknown, her essence pure.*
*Her laughter mixed with breathy sighs,*
*As he traced new treasures under soft skies.*
*Her waist became his holy grail,*
*A secret they shared, a whispered tale.*
*He kissed the mark, a silent pledge,*
*To love every inch, to cross every edge.*
*Their eyes met amidst the fervent embrace,*
*Speaking volumes without a race.*
*The mark of fascination was more than skin,*
*It unveiled emotions buried within.*
*For Pandey, it wasn't just physical bliss,*
*But the thrill of her essence in each kiss.*
*Her body, a map, her soul the terrain,*
*Every curve held mysteries to explain.*
*Vanya, too, found his fervor endearing,*
*His devotion pure, his touches searing.*
*Her mischievous grin returned anew,*
*As if daring him to find more clues.*

# CHAPTER SEVENTEEN

# The Aftermath of Bliss

*As dawn peeked gently, painting the skies,*
*The storm of passion began to subside.*
*The residue lingered, like an unspoken song,*
*Moments of heat where they both belonged.*
*Vanya's face, a canvas of blush and fire,*
*Held the tale of their shared desire.*
*Her wild laugh broke the morning's still,*
*A spark that Pandey could never will.*
*She sat in his shirt, oversized and loose,*
*The faintest hint of her scent infused.*
*Buttoned wrong in her hurried delight,*
*Yet, on her, it looked exquisitely right.*
*Her mischievous eyes met Pandey's bare chest,*
*A teasing glance, her gaze confessed.*
*"Shall I keep this shirt forever?" she dared,*
*As he stood shirtless, amused yet ensnared.*
*His laughter echoed, soft but sly,*
*"The shirt's yours, but I demand a reply.*
*What of my plight, left bare in the breeze?*
*Or should I roam like this with ease?"*
*Her fingers played at the hem of his shirt,*
*A naughty smirk, her charm expertly flirt.*
*She shrugged, feigning no concern at all,*
*"You're bold enough; no need to stall."*

*In the car's trunk lay his unsung savior,*
*An old, wrinkled tee of questionable flavor.*
*Pandey retrieved it, pulling it on with grace,*
*While her giggle danced across his face.*
*But her laughter wasn't merely for fun;*
*It carried the memory of what had begun.*
*The closeness shared, the boundaries erased,*
*The morning light glowing where passion embraced.*
*She tugged the sleeves of the shirt she wore,*
*Claiming it as hers, forevermore.*
*Pandey teased, "A thief in disguise?"*
*But her playful pout betrayed no lies.*
*"You've stolen my shirt, my peace, my heart,"*
*He said with a grin, playing his part.*
*"Keep them all, I'm left with less,*
*But a single smile of yours, I confess,*
*Can ransom me back, make me whole,*
*You've taken my shirt but claimed my soul."*
*She softened at that, her gaze more tender,*
*The night's wild heat now memories to remember.*
*The world outside seemed far away,*
*In their cocoon of love, they wished to stay.*
*Her hands reached for his, fingers entwined,*
*In that simple gesture, their hearts aligned.*
*"I may steal your shirts, your peace, your days,*
*But in return, Pandey, I promise to stay."*
*A promise veiled in playful prose,*
*In the aftermath of bliss, their love arose.*
*Not just a fleeting moment or night,*
*But a spark kindled into radiant light.*

# CHAPTER EIGHTEEN

# The Farewell & Keepsake

*The hostel gates loomed, stark and near,*
*Marking the end of a day held dear.*
*Their laughter lingered, the air still warm,*
*An echo of passion, a love yet to form.*
*Vanya stepped out, her steps so light,*
*Her presence a beacon in the velvet night.*
*The blue shirt she wore, loose and free,*
*Held the scent of Pandey, a silent decree.*
*He watched her leave, his heart ensnared,*
*By the moments they shared, the emotions declared.*
*The road stretched back, but he lingered there,*
*Lost in her aura, her smile, her care.*
*For this wasn't just a drive, a fleeting spree,*
*It was the start of something meant to be.*
*Their first adventure, raw and unplanned,*
*A tale of love, both wild and grand.*
*The shirt she wore wasn't just cloth,*
*It carried their story, tender and soft.*
*The memories etched in every thread,*
*Of laughter and kisses and words unsaid.*
*She turned for a moment, her eyes met his,*
*A fleeting glance, a parting bliss.*
*Her lips curled upward, a coy little grin,*

# A RELATIONSHIP OF SITUATIONSHIP

*As if to say, "This is where we begin."*
*And Pandey, though stoic, felt a swell,*
*A surge of emotions he couldn't quell.*
*For the shirt she carried wasn't just his,*
*It held their whispers, their stolen bliss.*
*The drive back alone, under moonlit skies,*
*Brought vivid flashes of her sleepy eyes.*
*The sound of her laughter, her soft little sighs,*
*Were etched in his mind, a love that defies.*
*The day played on, like a song on repeat,*
*The thrill of their closeness, her heartbeat.*
*The rain-soaked roads and the paneer pakora,*
*The chai that tasted of shared euphoria.*
*When he reached his room, her kurta remained,*
*A piece of her presence, the emotions ingrained.*
*He held it close, its folds held her scent,*
*A keepsake of moments, a day well spent.*
*And though the day ended, their bond unfurled,*
*A promise whispered to the listening world.*
*For love was brewing, steady and true,*
*In subtle gestures and skies so blue.*
*The memory of their drive would forever stay,*
*A chapter of sweetness, etched in the day.*
*For though no vows were spoken or made,*
*Their hearts had written a serenade.*
*The shirt and kurta were not mere attire,*
*They held the warmth of their shared desire.*
*A piece of her stayed, a piece of him went,*
*In that quiet exchange, their love was lent.*
*As Pandey lay in bed, the shirt still near,*
*He smiled at the thought, his feelings clear.*
*For their first long drive was not just a ride,*
*It was the start of love they couldn't hide.*

# CHAPTER NINETEEN

# A Rare Day of Seasons in Play

*It was one of those rare and mystical days,*
*When the seasons intertwined in curious ways.*
*The sun, regal, adorned the azure dome,*
*Its rays spilling warmth, a reminder of home.*
*Yet winter's whispers, quiet and soft,*
*Hinted of its arrival, the chill aloft.*
*A breath of frost in the afternoon air,*
*A prelude to change, a signal to prepare.*
*Summer, with all its fiery grace,*
*Bowed out gently, leaving no trace.*
*Its golden light, a fading glow,*
*Surrendered to autumn's cool, quiet flow.*
*The air turned crisp, with a playful bite,*
*The warmth of the sun, now a distant light.*
*Leaves pirouetted from the trees,*
*Spinning in the wind, caught in a breeze.*
*Golden and bold, they danced with ease,*
*Falling in silence, a delicate tease.*
*As autumn wrapped the world in its embrace,*
*The earth took on a soft, muted grace.*
*Flowers unfolded their secrets untold,*
*Delicate petals, hues of orange and gold.*
*The world seemed to pause, a perfect trance,*

*Caught between seasons, in a fleeting dance.*
*Pandey's room hummed with a vibrant tune,*
*A sanctuary of friends beneath a pale noon.*
*The air thick with stories, laughter, and cheer,*
*A safe haven of memories, precious and dear.*
*His friends lounged around, their voices a blend,*
*A collage of joy, with no need to pretend.*
*Tales were spun, and jokes took flight,*
*An orchestra of camaraderie, pure delight.*
*The air was alive with the comfort of sound,*
*As each moment lingered, perfectly unbound.*
*But amidst the revelry, the buzz and the chatter,*
*A chime broke through, cutting through the clatter.*
*The phone in his hand, with a familiar ring,*
*A melody that only she could bring.*
*"Pandey," she spoke, her voice like a plea,*
*Soft and warm, yet filled with urgency.*
*"Take me to the market, would you, for me?"*
*Her words, a request wrapped in tender grace,*
*Her quiet needs, written on her face.*
*A pause settled over him, the room's hum dulled,*
*As her voice tugged at his heart, it suddenly swelled.*
*A grin broke across his face, a knowing glance,*
*Their shared understanding, an unspoken dance.*
*Her gentle entreaty, simple yet clear,*
*Felt like a whisper only he could hear.*
*The friends around him, unaware of the shift,*
*Kept talking, but to him, it was a quiet rift.*
*He rose from the banter, a silent resolve,*
*As if the world around him began to evolve.*
*For Vanya's wishes, he seldom refused,*
*A truth unspoken, but deeply infused.*
*With every smile, every glance she gave,*
*He felt compelled to care, to be brave.*
*Her presence, like a melody, always so near,*

*Her wishes, a compass that he held dear.*
*The room's energy returned, but now he moved,*
*Driven by a call he'd never once disproved.*
*He grabbed his keys, his heart already racing,*
*Eager to fulfill the task, no time for pacing.*
*His friends cheered and waved him off with a grin,*
*For in Vanya's request, he always found win.*
*And so, with the autumn breeze in the air,*
*Pandey stepped out, his heart stripped bare.*
*Ready to give her whatever she might need,*
*For her smile was the light that made him proceed.*

# CHAPTER TWENTY

# The Vision at the Gate

*At the hostel gate, he waited in stride,*
*The chill of the morning, winter's bride.*
*A crispness in the air, as the world seemed to freeze,*
*But inside his chest, there was a different breeze.*
*The cold kissed his skin, but his heart burned warm,*
*For he knew she would come, like the dawn after storm.*
*Her presence, like sunlight breaking the gray,*
*Filling the world with warmth in a magical way.*
*And then, she appeared, in a flowing kurti white,*
*A vision transcendent, stealing the light.*
*Her silhouette danced in the pale morning glow,*
*Like a gentle breeze on freshly fallen snow.*
*Her steps were soft, yet filled with purpose and grace,*
*A quiet confidence etched upon her face.*
*Each movement was poetry, each glance a song,*
*As though she were where the universe belonged.*
*Every time he saw her, she seemed anew,*
*Like a changing landscape, a shifting hue.*
*One moment, a mystery wrapped in the night,*
*The next, a flame burning brilliantly bright.*
*She was both an enigma and an open book,*
*A story told in the curve of her look.*
*Her essence bore tales of mystery and grace,*
*A world of depth in every line of her face.*
*Each encounter etched her deeper in place,*

*As though time itself had slowed its pace.*
*Her eyes met his, and in that quiet gaze,*
*He saw a thousand untold stories, a thousand days.*
*Her lips curved, a silent hello,*
*A warmth amidst the winter's show.*
*It was a greeting unspoken, but understood,*
*A quiet reassurance that all was good.*
*Her presence, more than a moment in time,*
*It was a rhythm, a pulse, a quiet rhyme.*
*She moved towards him with effortless grace,*
*A soft smile lighting her delicate face.*
*Into the car, she gracefully slipped,*
*As though the world around them gently flipped.*
*The doors shut softly, sealing them in,*
*A new chapter beginning, where stories begin.*
*They sat in the car, the engine's hum low,*
*The world around them a steady, calm flow.*
*And into their adventure, they willingly dipped,*
*Together, as if fate had perfectly clipped*
*Their hearts in sync, their souls aligned,*
*Their paths, once separate, now intertwined.*
*The car sped forward, the city behind,*
*But in that moment, it was just them, entwined.*
*No past, no future, just this very now,*
*A perfect pause, the world was allowed to bow.*
*For in her presence, time held its breath,*
*And in his heart, there was nothing but depth.*
*They moved through the streets with no particular aim,*
*Their journey undefined, but never the same.*
*Each moment, a discovery, each glance, a spark,*
*Their connection glowing bright in the dark.*
*And in that moment, as the world spun around,*
*They were together, in perfect harmony, unbound.*

# CHAPTER TWENTY-ONE

# Market's Merriment and Mischief

*The market bustled, a cacophony alive,*
*A symphony of sounds, where life did thrive.*
*The chatter of vendors, the laughter of friends,*
*The rhythm of footsteps that never would end.*
*Yet in their bubble, amidst all the noise,*
*Only they existed, two souls in pure joy.*
*The colors around them, the scents in the air,*
*Felt like a dream, like a moment rare.*
*Through vibrant stalls, her list she pursued,*
*Her focus sharp, her gaze subdued.*
*Groceries, trinkets, and spices that gleamed,*
*Each item a treasure, as though she had dreamed.*
*The world swirled around them, chaotic and bright,*
*But in each other's company, everything felt right.*
*They moved through the market, a dance in their stride,*
*Each moment shared, a joy they couldn't hide.*
*They sampled street food, savoring the taste,*
*Each bite a memory they couldn't waste.*
*The tang of tamarind, the spice in the air,*
*Laughter shared, the simplest joy, so rare.*
*The night seemed to shimmer, under fairy lights,*
*The world turned softer, bathed in warm sights.*
*Their laughter echoed, blending with the sound,*

*Of the market's hum, of life all around.*
*Their hands brushed often, fingers entwined,*
*A touch so fleeting, yet perfectly timed.*
*It was as if the universe itself had conspired,*
*To bring them together, two hearts inspired.*
*No words needed, just a simple glance,*
*A connection unspoken, a perfect dance.*
*Each shared moment was a thread in the weave,*
*A bond so deep, it was hard to believe.*
*And then, as the market buzzed on in its way,*
*The mehndi stall caught Pandey's eye that day.*
*The vibrant colors, the intricate designs,*
*Pulled him in, as though fate had aligned.*
*His boyish mischief, that spark in his gaze,*
*Flickered to life in the market's maze.*
*"Let's do this!" he said, his spirit bright,*
*And his words were filled with that playful light.*
*Vanya raised an eyebrow, a smile on her lips,*
*Her heart racing slightly, her curiosity in grips.*
*The suddenness of it, the mischief so pure,*
*Was something in him she couldn't ignore.*
*Amused and intrigued, she couldn't fight,*
*The charm of his spirit, so effortlessly bright.*
*"Are you sure?" she asked, her voice light and teasing,*
*But her heart, she knew, was already pleasing.*
*With a laugh, he tugged her hand, leading the way,*
*To the stall where designs flourished and swayed.*
*The artist greeted them with a knowing smile,*
*As if she had seen this moment a while.*
*And so they sat, side by side in the glow,*
*Ready to create, ready to show*
*Their shared love for life, their bond so free,*
*With a dash of mischief, just as it should be.*
*As the mehndi swirled, their hands side by side,*
*A new connection formed, impossible to hide.*

*The intricate patterns, the dark henna stain,*
*Each line a story, a whisper, a chain.*
*Pandey's eyes sparkled with a mischievous gleam,*
*And Vanya, amused, was caught in the dream.*
*In that moment, amidst the crowd's hum,*
*They were simply together, where they'd both come.*
*The market alive, the night shining bright,*
*But in each other's presence, the world felt right.*

# CHAPTER TWENTY-TWO

# Art in Henna and Secrets to Keep

*She settled down, her palms outstretched,*
*The mehndi artist's craft freshly etched.*
*The cool paste spread across her skin,*
*A tapestry unfolding, a story within.*
*The intricate swirls, the delicate lines,*
*A dance of art, where tradition shines.*
*She watched in silence as the artist worked,*
*Each stroke of henna a promise, unspoken, yet lurked.*
*Pandey browsed designs, elaborate and grand,*
*His eyes scanning the options, hand in hand.*
*He marveled at the patterns meant for a bride,*
*Each one a symbol, with meaning implied.*
*He paused at a design, so bold and so true,*
*A delicate floral pattern, intricate and new.*
*But his eyes darted, unsure of the choice,*
*Seeking Vanya's opinion, her guiding voice.*
*Vanya chuckled, her eyes aglow,*
*At Pandey's innocence, his playful show.*
*His unsure expression, so endearing and sweet,*
*A boy who wore his heart on his sleeve, so neat.*
*She couldn't help but smile, her gaze soft and kind,*
*Watching him try, with a curious mind.*
*But beneath her smile, a scheme did hide,*

*A playful thought that she couldn't confide.*
*Her lips curled with mischief, eyes sparkling bright,*
*A plan began to form, perfect in its light.*
*"Fetch me nail paint," she cleverly bid,*
*Her tone sweet and casual, a hint to be hid.*
*He glanced at her, unsure of the need,*
*But her smile was all he could heed.*
*"Of course!" he replied, eager to aid,*
*His loyalty to her in every step laid.*
*As he stepped away, to fetch her request,*
*Vanya's mind danced with a plan, manifest.*
*Alone with the artist, she whispered low,*
*Her voice a secret, only they'd know.*
*"Write his name where the patterns flow,"*
*A quiet command, a soft undertone,*
*A playful idea, a gesture profound,*
*A touch of mischief that would soon be found.*
*The artist paused, her hands steady and sure,*
*She nodded, understanding the allure.*
*With a quiet smile, she set to work,*
*In the design, she wove a hidden perk.*
*A name, so simple, yet full of heart,*
*In the midst of the patterns, a subtle start.*
*Pandey's name, like a whisper, was drawn,*
*A secret sealed within the dawn.*
*Vanya's eyes sparkled, a satisfaction deep,*
*As the artist worked, the plan hers to keep.*
*She leaned back, her smile a soft, knowing curve,*
*For the surprise she planned, he'd surely observe.*
*The patterns grew, delicate and fine,*
*But it was the name hidden that would soon shine.*
*Pandey returned, the nail paint in hand,*
*Unaware of the trick, of the hidden strand.*
*He sat beside her, watching in awe,*
*At the art on her hands, every flaw.*

*And as the henna dried, he couldn't help but stare,*
*At the beauty unfolding, at the love in the air.*
*But what he didn't know, what remained unseen,*
*Was the name etched beneath the intricate sheen.*
*Her playful secret, her quiet surprise,*
*A gift that would glimmer beneath her guise.*
*And as their eyes met, she couldn't resist,*
*The glint of mischief that she couldn't dismiss.*

# An Evening Painted in Henna

*As the evening fell, the work was done,*
*The henna dried beneath the setting sun.*
*The world around them softened, kissed by twilight,*
*A gentle calmness, a cool embrace of night.*
*The vibrant market now a distant hum,*
*Their journey concluded, the day almost numb.*
*Their errands complete, they made their way,*
*To her hostel gate at the close of day.*
*The air, still crisp with the whisper of night,*
*Brought a sense of peace, a quiet delight.*
*"Look at my hands," she said with pride,*
*Her voice a mix of joy and mischief, side by side.*
*Pandey turned, his eyes soft with affection,*
*Admiring her beauty with tender reflection.*
*He leaned in close, drawn by the glow,*
*Her hands like an artwork, a story to show.*
*The intricate patterns, bold and neat,*
*Each curve and swirl, so complete.*
*But something hidden made his heart beat,*
*A quiet realization, soft but sweet.*
*As he gazed, his eyes traced the design,*
*A subtle detail, a secret line.*
*There it was, within the elegant flow,*

*His name, a hidden truth only they'd know.*
*The henna, a canvas of memories shared,*
*A hidden declaration, a promise declared.*
*His pulse quickened, a flicker of surprise,*
*The warmth of it spreading, right in his eyes.*
*It was more than just art, more than a game,*
*It was a gesture, a symbol, an unspoken claim.*
*A soft smile tugged at the corner of his lips,*
*As his heart danced with gentle flips.*
*For the name etched within the design,*
*Felt like a bond, a sign, divine.*
*A flicker of warmth, a stirring of grace,*
*Reflected in her mischievous face.*
*Her eyes twinkled, like stars in the night,*
*A playful glimmer, soft and bright.*
*She knew the effect, she knew the power,*
*Her secret hidden, like a blooming flower.*
*With a casual air, she held his gaze,*
*But the truth between them set the world ablaze.*
*Pandey's fingers brushed her palm, so light,*
*As if the name written there brought them to flight.*
*He smiled, an expression that spoke so clear,*
*His heart, now full, no longer in fear.*
*The simple gesture had shifted the air,*
*Binding them closer with a thread so rare.*
*The mystery of her had unraveled in time,*
*Her heart now entwined with his, sublime.*
*As the night deepened, the stars shone above,*
*Their hands, their hearts, wrapped in a new love.*
*The world around them faded, just a blur,*
*For in this moment, it was only them, a whisper, a stir.*
*And though no words were spoken aloud,*
*Their connection was strong, both quiet and proud.*
*For her secret, etched in henna's embrace,*
*Had sealed their bond in time and space.*

# CHAPTER TWENTY-FOUR

# A Kiss & A Memory

*Before he could speak, her lips found his,*
*A fleeting moment, a stolen bliss.*
*It was quick, yet timeless, a spark in the air,*
*A kiss that whispered secrets, tender and rare.*
*His heart skipped, unsure of what had just been,*
*A sudden connection, a spark within.*
*Her lips, warm and soft, a promise in disguise,*
*That lingered long after she pulled away, shy.*
*She laughed, a sound like wind through trees,*
*Her spirit free, carried on the breeze.*
*With a mischievous grin, she turned on her heel,*
*Disappearing into the night, with a joy so real.*
*Leaving Pandey standing there, his mind a swirl,*
*Caught in the wake of this whirlwind girl.*
*Her presence, a flame that had burned so bright,*
*Now fading softly into the night.*
*He lingered there, by her hostel gate,*
*Lost in the spell of unexpected fate.*
*The kiss, the laughter, the playful tease,*
*Were like fragments of a dream, too sweet to seize.*
*His mind raced, trying to piece it all together,*
*What was it? Was it love, or just a fleeting tether?*
*The world around him felt distant and strange,*
*Like he was suspended, caught in a change.*

*A cigarette lit, its smoke a haze,*
*Curling into the cool evening's maze.*
*He took a slow drag, the embers burning bright,*
*As he tried to shake off the feeling of the night.*
*The smoke swirled in the air, like his thoughts,*
*Chasing after the mystery that time forgot.*
*Each inhale a quiet moment, each exhale a sigh,*
*A way to steady his pulse, to quiet the high.*
*He replayed the enchantment of the day,*
*Her eyes, her laugh, the words they didn't say.*
*The way she moved, so effortlessly free,*
*Like she was a part of the world, wild and untamed, just like the sea.*
*Her touch, her smile, like a spell cast in time,*
*Leaving him in awe, caught in her rhyme.*
*A smile tugged at the corner of his lips,*
*As he shook his head, taking another sip.*
*Pandey leaned against the cold brick wall,*
*His thoughts echoing, a constant call.*
*He wasn't sure what it meant, this feeling inside,*
*But he knew he couldn't hide.*
*Something had shifted, something had changed,*
*A door had opened, their worlds rearranged.*
*As the night grew darker, the streetlights flickered on,*
*Pandey stayed there, thinking of her, long after she was gone.*
*The kiss, the laughter, the freedom she held,*
*Now etched in his heart, a story to be quelled.*
*And though the world continued to spin,*
*He knew this moment would linger, deep within.*

# CHAPTER TWENTY-FIVE

# Reflections in the Night

*Back in his room, beneath the stars' light,*
*Pandey recalled the magical night.*
*The moon hung high, casting silver beams,*
*As his mind replayed the dance of their dreams.*
*Her laughter, a melody, soft and free,*
*A sound that lingered, like a breeze through a tree.*
*Her charm, unspoken yet loud in its way,*
*A presence that had brightened the dullest of days.*
*The name in her henna, a secret so sweet,*
*Tucked in the curves of the patterns' heartbeat.*
*He could still see it, etched in his mind,*
*A symbol of something deeper to find.*
*A story etched in fragrant aroma,*
*The scent of spices, warmth, and sweet karma.*
*It was more than just art, more than a game,*
*It was a connection, no need to explain.*
*For in her simplicity, she had concealed,*
*A love profound, slowly revealed.*
*Hidden beneath the laughter and playful tease,*
*Was a tenderness that put his heart at ease.*
*The way she moved, the way she spoke,*
*Each glance a mystery, each smile bespoke.*
*Her wild spirit, her gentle grace,*
*In her, he found a perfect place.*

*And as he drifted into a dreamful embrace,*
*His thoughts of her, he couldn't erase.*
*The quiet whisper of her name,*
*A sweet refrain, like a soft flame.*
*He carried her essence, her laugh, her grace,*
*A love unfurling in the quiet space.*
*The night grew still, the world outside,*
*But within him, emotions began to collide.*
*She had opened a door, one he hadn't known,*
*And now, with each thought, he was not alone.*
*He could feel her presence, warm and near,*
*A comforting thought, one he held dear.*
*As he closed his eyes, the room felt small,*
*But within his heart, she filled it all.*
*The kiss, the name, the way she moved,*
*Were pieces of a puzzle that he now approved.*
*A love, so new, yet strangely known,*
*A bond that, in his soul, had already grown.*
*In the quiet of night, he let out a sigh,*
*And whispered her name, as the moments flew by.*
*For as sleep took him, soft and slow,*
*He knew in his heart, this love would grow.*

# CHAPTER TWENTY-SIX

# Through Unknown Roads: A Love That Dared

*It was one of those rare winter mornings when the sun lingered in the sky, yet the air held a biting chill. The semester at college had come to a close, and the students were scattering, returning to their homes to bask in the brief holiday before exams loomed. Among them was Vanya, who had gone back to her hometown of Saharanpur. Pandey, however, was left behind, tethered to the campus by unfinished practical work that demanded his attention.*

*Pandey sat at his desk, a collection of files and papers spread before him. His mind, however, was elsewhere. He had been calling Vanya since morning, but her phone remained silent. She was still asleep, oblivious to his attempts to reach her. With a sigh, Pandey resolved to finish his work and headed to the college to submit his practical. By the time he was done, it was past noon, and his mood was far from ideal. He decided to grab some food from a nearby restaurant, hoping to lift his spirits.*

*As he drove to the restaurant, a sudden thought struck him. What if he visited Saharanpur? The idea was impulsive, reckless even, but it gripped him with an unshakable intensity. He had never been to Saharanpur, never taken those roads, and the journey was unfamiliar territory. Yet, the prospect of seeing Vanya outweighed any hesitation. Without second thoughts, Pandey rerouted his car, embarking on the three-hour drive to an unknown destination.*

*The highway stretched before him, an endless ribbon flanked by fields and trees. The journey took him through villages, past a dam, and across agricultural expanses that painted the landscape in hues of green and brown. It was a picturesque route, but Pandey was too preoccupied to fully appreciate it. As he drove, his phone finally rang. It was Vanya.*

*His heart skipped a beat as he answered, unsure of how to explain his actions. "Hey," he said, keeping his voice casual. "Just submitted my practicals. Heading out for some lunch." He didn't mention that he hadn't eaten a thing all day or that he was currently halfway to her city. Vanya, unaware of his plan, chatted briefly before hanging up.*

*As the signal faded while he crossed a remote village, Pandey realized he had lost his way. The roads seemed to blur into one another, and without a clear direction, he began to feel the weight of his decision. Yet, determination pushed him forward. After a series of wrong turns and a growing sense of frustration, he finally found his way back to the highway. The GPS signal returned, and his destination was now just 50 kilometers away.*

*But another hurdle awaited him: he had no idea where Vanya lived. His mind raced as he tried to remember if she had ever mentioned her address. Then it struck him—the college portal might have her details. Pulling over, he searched the student database and found her address: Mahavir Colony. Relief washed over him, mingling with a renewed sense of anxiety and excitement.*

*As he neared Mahavir Colony, every emotion imaginable coursed through him. Excitement, nervousness, joy, and a tinge of fear all collided within his chest. Parking outside the gated society, he tried calling Vanya again, but her phone remained unanswered. Residents eyed him curiously, an unfamiliar car and a stranger in their midst. Uncomfortable under their scrutiny, Pandey decided to enter the colony and locate her house himself.*

*He drove slowly, scanning the houses until one caught his eye. It was familiar, a house he had seen in pictures Vanya had shared. His heart raced as he parked outside. What now? Should he knock on the door? Call her again? Instead, he opted for a video call.*

*Vanya answered, her face sleepy but cheerful. "Hey, Pandey! What's up?" she asked, stretching.*

*"How are you? Feeling rested?" he replied, trying to sound casual. As they talked, he flipped the camera, revealing the house behind him. For a moment, Vanya didn't react, but then realization dawned. Her eyes widened as she recognized her home on the screen. "Wait... what?" she stammered before abruptly ending the call.*

*Moments later, Vanya appeared on the balcony, scanning the street. Her gaze fell on Pandey's car, and her expression shifted from shock to disbelief. She descended slowly, her movements deliberate, a mix of emotions playing on her face. When she reached the car, she opened the door and slid into the passenger seat.*

*"Pandey," she began, her voice a mixture of admonishment and affection. "What are you doing here?"*

*Before he could answer, she hugged him tightly. Then, just as suddenly, she pulled back and slapped his arm. "You're crazy! Do you know how reckless this is?"*

*Pandey laughed, a nervous yet genuine sound. "I missed you," he admitted simply.*

*Her eyes softened, tears welling up as she smiled. "You're impossible."*

*They sat there for an hour, talking about everything and nothing. She laughed, cried, teased, and scolded him, her emotions a whirlwind. It was a moment Pandey would treasure forever, a culmination of his impromptu journey and the emotions that had driven him there.*

*As the evening approached, it was time for Pandey to head back. He hugged Vanya tightly, their connection deepened by the day's events. She kissed him on the cheek, a gesture of affection and gratitude, before waving him off.*

*The drive back was quiet, the roads still unfamiliar. Pandey replayed the day in his mind, a smile lingering on his lips. But his journey took an unexpected turn when, thirty minutes in, one of his tires punctured. Stranded on the highway, he assessed the damage and realized he would have to walk to find a repair shop.*

*He called Vanya to let her know, assuring her he was fine. Despite her worry, he managed to calm her down. Carrying the damaged tire, Pandey walked three kilometers to a small shop where a mechanic patched it up. The ordeal was exhausting, but Pandey didn't mind. The memory of Vanya's smile and the warmth of her hug made every hardship worthwhile.*

*It was late when he finally returned to his room. He reheated some leftovers and ate in silence, his thoughts still lingering on the day. Though tired, he felt an overwhelming sense of contentment. The surprise visit, the long drive, and the challenges along the way had all been worth it. For Pandey, seeing Vanya was more than just a spontaneous decision; it was a reaffirmation of the love he held for her, a love that made every risk and every effort feel insignificant in comparison.*

# CHAPTER TWENTY-SEVEN

# A Birthday Tale Under Winter's Veil

*It was February—a month of love and whispered grace,*
*When winter adorned the earth in its icy embrace.*
*The days were short, the nights serene,*
*And Pandey's birthday lay waiting, unseen.*
*The sixteenth was his date of birth,*
*But for Pandey, it held little mirth.*
*To him, the day was like any other,*
*No grand parade, no joy to uncover.*
*Vanya, though, had a different plan,*
*To celebrate the quiet, thoughtful man.*
*She sought the help of Avi, his friend,*
*To make the night one he'd treasure till the end.*
*As the clock crept close to midnight's song,*
*Pandey lay resting, the night stretched long.*
*He'd spoken to Vanya, her voice like balm,*
*Her gentle tones, his heart's true calm.*
*"Goodnight, Buu," she'd softly said,*
*And to his slumber, Pandey was led.*
*Yet elsewhere, Vanya stirred with delight,*
*For her surprise would unfold that very night.*

# CHAPTER TWENTY-EIGHT

# The Midnight Surprise

*At twelve past fifteen, the clock did chime,*
*And Avi stepped into Pandey's time.*
*With a mischievous grin and a glint in his eye,*
*He entered the room, the moment to amplify.*
*In his hands, a cake aglow,*
*A butterscotch delight, its candles a show.*
*The flicker of light danced in the dark,*
*As if the cake itself held a spark.*
*The room filled with warmth, the scent so sweet,*
*A birthday surprise, a moment complete.*
*"Happy Birthday, Buu!" Vanya's voice rang clear,*
*Through a video call, her laughter sincere.*
*Her face, bright with joy, beamed through the screen,*
*A connection so strong, despite the unseen.*
*Pandey, startled, his eyes half-closed,*
*Had been pulled from slumber, his mind still composed.*
*His heart, still heavy with dreams and haze,*
*Felt the weight of her love in unexpected ways.*
*He blinked at the cake, the light shining bright,*
*And found himself grounded in this pure delight.*
*A smile crept across his sleepy face,*
*His shyness masked in a moment's grace.*
*There was something in her voice, so sweet,*
*That made his heart skip a beat.*
*The world around him seemed to fade,*

*As Vanya's words in his mind replayed.*
*Her laughter was a melody, a song so true,*
*A reminder of how much he cherished her too.*
*Yet, though the cake was sweet and fine,*
*Pandey knew he couldn't cross the line.*
*For milk and he were a warring pair,*
*A single bite—he wouldn't dare.*
*His throat, once caught in the milk's embrace,*
*Would rebel in fury, his face an unwelcome trace.*
*But how could he explain, in this moment so pure,*
*That the cake she brought was something to endure?*
*Vanya, unaware of his plight,*
*Had chosen the cake to bring him delight.*
*Her gesture, so simple, so full of care,*
*Made him feel like he was floating in air.*
*But the cake's milk base, a hidden curse,*
*Made Pandey's dilemma grow worse.*
*Yet, what could he do? What could he say?*
*Not when she was so far away.*
*He took a piece, small and neat,*
*And ate it for her, his love complete.*
*The flavor danced, sweet on his tongue,*
*Though his body rebelled, his thoughts were young.*
*For Vanya's joy was worth the cost,*
*Even if the price was moments lost.*
*He chewed with care, his face a mask,*
*Hoping she wouldn't ask.*
*"Why didn't you tell me?" she cried in dismay,*
*"You're allergic to this, and yet you obey?"*
*Her voice, a mix of shock and concern,*
*Made Pandey's heart twist, and his stomach churn.*
*She could see through the charade, the way he tried,*
*To hide the discomfort he couldn't deny.*
*His silence spoke volumes, his love so clear,*
*That he'd go through anything, just to have her near.*

*"But why, Pandey?" she asked again,*
*Her eyes wide with worry, her brow a gentle strain.*
*He smiled softly, brushing it off,*
*Not wanting her to feel the sting, the cough.*
*"It's nothing," he muttered, with a casual air,*
*A gesture of strength, though he didn't care.*
*What mattered most, what he couldn't say,*
*Was how much he loved her in every way.*
*He reached out to the screen, his fingers light,*
*And in the moment, everything felt right.*
*Her face, the way she worried for him,*
*Made his heart ache, a love so dim.*
*Pandey would endure, as he always did,*
*For her happiness, he'd never hid.*
*He was hers in that moment, no more, no less,*
*The milk, the cake, nothing could suppress.*

# CHAPTER TWENTY-NINE

# Pandey's Words

*Her tears fell soft, her worry immense,*
*But Pandey's words were a soothing defense.*
*He saw the concern in her eyes so bright,*
*Her love, her care, a guiding light.*
*Pandey, always reserved, his heart tucked away,*
*Found the courage to speak in the most unexpected way.*
*"How could I not, when it's for you?*
*This cake is more than a dessert to chew."*
*His voice was gentle, wrapped in truth,*
*A softness in his words, an unspoken proof.*
*He spun a tale, a magician of words,*
*Each phrase a melody, like singing birds.*
*His words took flight, as if they were wings,*
*Carrying them both to unknown things.*
*He spoke of stars and the moonlit sea,*
*Of how her love was his jubilee.*
*How her laughter was the rhythm to his heart,*
*A song that never would depart.*
*Her presence, the sunrise after the rain,*
*A cure for every bit of his pain.*
*"What's a moment's discomfort," he said with a grin,*
*"When your joy is the prize I win?"*
*His eyes sparkled, his smile so warm,*
*A moment of calm in the midst of the storm.*
*His words wove a tapestry of delight,*

*Chasing away the shadows of the night.*
*Her worry, her doubt, began to fade,*
*Replaced by a warmth that the night had made.*
*Her tears dissolved, replaced by a smile,*
*His charm had softened her heart's denial.*
*The sadness lifted, like fog in the light,*
*And in its place, everything felt right.*
*Pandey watched as her face softened, bright,*
*Her worry melting like snow in the sunlight.*
*She wiped her eyes, a smile breaking through,*
*And in that moment, their bond only grew.*
*"You always know how to make it better," she said,*
*Her voice now calm, her fears misled.*
*Pandey chuckled, the twinkle in his eye,*
*As he brushed the last of her tears goodbye.*
*He reached for her, his touch so light,*
*As if to hold her in the soft, moonlit night.*
*"No need for thanks, not for something so small,*
*I'd do anything to see you stand tall."*
*The cake, the milk, and all the fuss,*
*Became nothing in the glow of this trust.*
*It was her smile, her happiness, that he craved,*
*Her joy, her peace—these were what he saved.*
*Pandey, the quiet, the one who hid,*
*Had let his heart speak, and it was no longer rid*
*Of the feelings he'd locked away for so long—*
*Now, he knew where his heart truly belonged.*

# The Night Wanes On

*Avi departed, his mission complete,*
*Leaving the lovers in a connection sweet.*
*The video call lingered, their voices low,*
*As the hours ticked by, their faces aglow.*
*They spoke of dreams, of days to come,*
*Of laughter shared and battles won.*
*Their love, a tapestry woven tight,*
*Grew richer still in the quiet night.*
*Eyes heavy, they drifted to sleep,*
*Together in dreams, their bond to keep.*
*The call remained, their screens aglow,*
*Two hearts tethered, letting love grow.*

# CHAPTER THIRTY-ONE

# A Morning Full of Warmth

*The dawn broke gently, winter's chill,*
*Yet Pandey's heart was warm and still.*
*The sky, painted with hues of gold,*
*Whispered secrets of the day to unfold.*
*The memories of the midnight past,*
*Etched in his soul, forever to last.*
*Each moment, a thread in the tapestry bright,*
*A story written in the quiet of night.*
*Her laughter, her care, still echoed in his mind,*
*A love so pure, so gently entwined.*
*Though he'd never sought birthday cheer,*
*Vanya's gesture made the day dear.*
*For Pandey, birthdays were just another day,*
*A simple pause in life's endless sway.*
*But Vanya, with her warmth, had brought him light,*
*Turning his world from dark to bright.*
*A simple cake, a heartfelt call,*
*Transformed the day into a carnival.*
*The sweet surprise, the love unspoken,*
*Had made his heart feel wide open.*
*For love isn't grand, nor loud in its say,*
*It's the little things that light the way.*
*The quiet moments, the tender glance,*
*The unexpected touch, the stolen chance.*
*It's not the fireworks that light the sky,*

*But the whispered words, the reasons why.*
*In the smallest gestures, the sweetest grace,*
*Love finds its way, it carves its place.*
*And as Pandey rose to greet the sun,*
*He knew this chapter was just begun.*
*The morning light, soft and pure,*
*Filled him with hope, a love so sure.*
*He felt it deep, in every beat,*
*In the rhythm of his heart, steady and sweet.*
*For something had shifted, something had grown,*
*In his chest, a warmth he'd never known.*
*The cake, the laughter, the shared embrace,*
*Had set a new course, a different pace.*
*No longer afraid to open his heart,*
*Pandey felt the world begin to restart.*
*The day was fresh, the air crisp and clear,*
*And Vanya's presence felt ever near.*
*He knew that the future was theirs to write,*
*A journey that would be filled with light.*
*As he stepped outside, his thoughts ran deep,*
*A promise to himself, a vow to keep.*
*For love, though quiet, though soft in its art,*
*Had made its home inside his heart.*
*And with every step, with every breath,*
*Pandey knew this was love's first depth.*
*He was ready now, to see what would come,*
*For in this new chapter, he wasn't alone.*

# CHAPTER THIRTY-TWO

# The Everyday Symphony

*As days turned to weeks and weeks to years,*
*Their bond grew strong amidst hidden fears.*
*The quiet love that neither had voiced,*
*Ached in the silence, but neither rejoiced.*
*For love, unspoken, can bear its weight,*
*A heavy crown or a fickle fate.*
*It lingered between them, tender yet true,*
*A longing unspoken, neither knew what to do.*
*They danced around it, with every glance,*
*A love so deep, but never by chance.*
*To college they'd ride, her hands on his waist,*
*Moments fleeting, too sweet to waste.*
*Through crowded streets and morning haze,*
*They traveled together, their hearts ablaze.*
*In the stillness of dawn, before the world awoke,*
*Pandey's heart fluttered, words still unspoke.*
*Her presence beside him, calm and serene,*
*Made the chaos of life feel like a dream.*
*In her eyes, he found his peace,*
*A place where all his worries ceased.*
*The mess's food, the chai they'd share,*
*All became treasures, beyond compare.*
*The taste of the chai, too sweet, too strong,*
*A symbol of the moments where they belonged.*
*Laughter spilled over the plastic cups,*

*In the little things, their love would erupt.*
*They'd argue over the spices, the flavors just right,*
*Finding comfort in the simplest of sights.*
*Each cup a promise, each sip a bond,*
*A connection that grew deeper, yet beyond.*
*In the crowded mess, in the bustling hall,*
*They carved out a space where nothing felt small.*
*Their love was not loud, not seen from afar,*
*But it was there in the quiet, under every star.*
*The hurried lunches, the late-night talks,*
*The long walks home in the dark, calm walks.*
*She'd lean on him, her head on his shoulder,*
*The years passing by, their hearts growing bolder.*
*The love they nurtured was woven with care,*
*With moments stolen, with time to spare.*
*Though neither had said it, neither had spoken,*
*The silence between them was more than a token.*
*For in that quiet, in every shared glance,*
*Their hearts had found a rare kind of dance.*
*And as the years unfurled with tender grace,*
*Pandey knew that love had found its place.*
*In the rhythm of their days, in the echoes of laughter,*
*They knew they'd cherish this bond long after.*
*A love not spoken, but felt in each breath,*
*Stronger than words, defying time and death.*

# CHAPTER THIRTY-THREE

# Whispers Of Three Days of Fire and Forever Love

*As days melted into memories and moments intertwined like strands of silk, Pandey and Vanya's bond evolved into something ethereal. What had begun as friendship had blossomed into a deep, unspoken connection — one that neither could deny. They were best friends who had found love in the purest corners of their hearts, their souls drawn together by an invisible thread, woven with laughter, shared secrets, and the silent understanding that transcended words. Their connection was an intoxicating mix of innocence and desire, where every glance, every touch, every word carried an unspoken promise of forever. It was a love that didn't need to be declared aloud because they both knew it in the deepest parts of their being.*

*There were mornings where the sun painted their world with a soft glow, and their simple exchanges felt like a warm embrace. In the rush of college life, they were each other's refuge, a sanctuary where they could just be — no pretense, no expectations. The way they fit together was effortless, like two pieces of a puzzle that had been waiting for years to find one another.*

*The semester's end brought a new kind of freedom, as the campus emptied out, and the usual chaos of assignments and deadlines gave way to the quiet hum of anticipation. Examinations had drawn to a close, their marks already forgotten, and a stretch of holidays lay ahead, filled with the promise of rest, reflection, and new adventures. The weight of the academic year lifted, and the world seemed to open* up in front of them.

Vanya, like the vibrant soul she was, had already begun packing, preparing for her departure to her hometown of Saharanpur. Her room, once filled with the clutter of textbooks, now held only the essentials — a suitcase, some clothes, and memories of a year well-lived. Yet, beneath her usual chatter and laughter, something stirred within her — a quiet restlessness that was impossible to ignore. The thought of leaving Pandey, even for a short time, unsettled her in a way she hadn't anticipated. She had always been independent, strong-willed, yet this bond between them had shifted something deep within her heart. She realized, in the stillness of those final days on campus, that she couldn't just walk away without one last moment — one last stolen piece of time where they could be completely, utterly theirs.

A plan began to form, something that danced between rebellion and romance, between a quiet defiance of routine and a desire to fully embrace what they had. Vanya was determined — no, resolute — to spend a few uninterrupted days with Pandey before she returned to her family. She had thought about it long into the night, after the others had gone to bed, and each moment of quiet contemplation had only fueled her resolve. The idea felt exhilarating, like a secret adventure waiting to be explored, something that would be entirely theirs.

Her heart beat with the rhythm of anticipation. It wasn't just about a few carefree days together; it was about more than that. It was about taking the space to savor what they had, to explore it deeper before the world pulled them in different directions again. Vanya knew that life, with all its unpredictability, would eventually change them, but for now, she wanted this moment — this beautiful pause in time — to be theirs and theirs alone.

She moved through her packing with a sense of purpose, her fingers lightly brushing over the items she was placing in her bag, but her mind was already miles ahead. She could already picture the quiet mornings, the conversations that would stretch into the night, the way Pandey's smile would light up the room when he realized what she was planning. There was a thrill in her chest, a sense of rebellion against *the inevitable return to her family, yet there was also a deep yearning for something lasting, something that only time could create. She knew that no matter how far apart they would be in the coming weeks, this bond would continue to grow, anchored in the quiet moments they had shared.*

*And as she zipped up the last of her bags, the plan she had made, bold and unspoken, began to take shape. She was ready to make that moment happen, to make the days before her departure something she would carry with her forever.*

*Vanya's resolve was unwavering, her heart full of anticipation, her eyes sparkling with the secret of what was to come. And as the last traces of the semester's chaos faded into the past, the real adventure — the one of love, of moments stolen and cherished — was only just beginning.*

# CHAPTER THIRTY-FOUR

# The Plan

*Vanya had always been a master of improvisation, a skill she had honed over the years, and this time was no different. She knew how to weave stories, to bend the truth just enough to make it believable. There was an art to it, a finesse she wielded effortlessly. For the past few days, she had been quietly orchestrating a plan, crafting the perfect ruse to ensure that no one — especially her family — would suspect that she had no intention of returning to Saharanpur anytime soon.*

*With the precision of a seasoned strategist, she enlisted the help of her cousins and roommate, each one unknowingly playing their part in her little game. Train tickets were booked for a departure that never truly existed, and a call was made to her family, assuring them that she would be on her way home within three days. She even made sure to share the details with the hostel staff, ensuring that no one would question her sudden absence. But Vanya's heart was set on a different destination — a place where the hum of the world fell silent, where only the pulse of her love for Pandey mattered. Her heart longed for his presence, and nothing, not even the expectations of family, could stand in her way.*

*When the day finally arrived, Pandey was, as always, his composed self. He had no inkling of the storm brewing in Vanya's mind, nor the secret journey they were about to embark on. He arrived at the hostel, as promised, to pick her up. His car was loaded with her bags, each one filled with the promise of a departure — a departure that was supposed to be a goodbye, a farewell to the life they had shared in* college. The drive to the railway station was nothing out of the ordinary, filled with their usual banter.

Pandey hummed along to the radio, making casual conversation about nothing in particular, while Vanya's laughter rang through the air like a melody. Yet, if he had paid closer attention, he would have noticed the subtle glint of mischief in her eyes, a spark that hinted at something more — something beyond the familiar rhythm of their conversations. But he didn't. He was too wrapped up in the comfort of her presence, in the ease with which they moved through life together.

As they neared the railway station, Vanya, ever the one to chase adventure in the smallest of moments, suggested that they stop at a nearby restaurant. Her tone was light, playful, and yet there was something in her voice that made it impossible for Pandey to resist. It was a suggestion that seemed harmless enough, a simple detour before she boarded her train. But, unbeknownst to him, it was the first step in her plan — a plan that would take them far from the station and from the lives they had known.

"Let's just grab a bite before I go," she urged, her eyes twinkling with an unspoken promise. Pandey, ever enchanted by her spirit, agreed without hesitation, happy to indulge her whims as he always did.

The restaurant was quiet, a small oasis nestled on the edge of the busy road. They settled into a cozy booth, the world outside fading away as their conversation flowed effortlessly, the same as it always had. Vanya's laughter, her teasing remarks, and Pandey's gentle responses filled the air. He was lost in the rhythm of their easy companionship, savoring the warmth of her presence. Yet there was a lingering feeling in the pit of his stomach, a subtle unease that he couldn't quite place.

It was in these moments, the ones where time slowed down, that Vanya's plan began to unfold. Each passing minute, each stolen glance, brought them closer to the moment when everything would change. She watched him, her heart swelling with affection, knowing that the truth would soon be revealed.

*Pandey was still blissfully unaware, caught up in the mundane beauty of their shared moments. But Vanya's heart raced, her thoughts spinning with excitement and fear. She was taking a leap of faith, stepping into unknown territory, but she couldn't help it. She wanted this, wanted him, wanted to break free from the life she had been leading, if only for a few stolen days.*

*As they finished their meal, she couldn't stop the grin that spread across her face. She was on the edge of something, something thrilling, and there was no turning back. Every second with Pandey felt like it was stretching into eternity, and in that moment, she realized that no matter where life would take them, these moments — these stolen days — would be the ones she'd carry with her forever.*

*And so, as the meal came to an end, the day began to shift. Vanya was no longer just a girl saying goodbye; she was someone who was stepping into the unknown, with Pandey by her side. What started as a casual detour had morphed into a turning point, and with one final glance at him, her heart racing, she knew that soon enough, the revelation would come. The direction of their days, and their lives, would never be the same again.*

# CHAPTER THIRTY-FIVE

# The Revelation

*As they reached the railway station and parked in the crowded lot, Pandey turned to help Vanya with her backpack. But she stopped him, her hand firm yet trembling against his. "Pandey, come closer," she whispered, her voice a mixture of urgency and affection.*

*Confused, Pandey leaned in, and before he could process what was happening, Vanya pressed her lips to his cheek. "I'm not going anywhere," she murmured against his skin, her words vibrating with emotion.*

*His eyes widened in disbelief. "What do you mean, Vanya? Your train..."*

*"My train can wait," she interrupted, her smile mischievous. She then explained her carefully laid plan, her excitement spilling over like a rushing stream. Pandey's initial reaction was a blend of shock and exasperation, but her infectious enthusiasm soon melted his resolve.*

*"You're crazy, Vanya," he said, shaking his head with a mix of amusement and affection. "But I'm glad you're my kind of crazy."*

# CHAPTER THIRTY-SIX

# A New Destination

*With the station fading in the rearview mirror and the promise of a weekend ahead, Pandey and Vanya were finally heading into uncharted territory. The train station, once a symbol of separation and fleeting goodbyes, now felt distant, as though they had crossed an invisible line into something entirely new. They had made a choice, one that neither of them had fully prepared for, but both were too curious to back out of now.*

*For the next three days, they would be away from the world they knew — a world that consisted of campus halls, classmates, and routines. Instead, they had retreated to a modest hotel, a quiet sanctuary tucked away in the midst of the city. The simple act of booking a room together was thrilling for both of them, though the excitement was tinged with a slight undercurrent of nervousness. For Pandey, the idea was especially daunting. He had always been a private person, careful with his actions, and the thought of being seen here, with Vanya, caused a ripple of apprehension. He was known around the city — not just by his friends but by acquaintances and strangers alike — and the possibility of being recognized made him uneasy. But for once, that didn't matter. What mattered was the time they had, away from prying eyes, away from expectations.*

*The hotel room was a cozy little space, simple but intimate. Soft lighting hung from the ceiling, casting a warm, golden glow over the room, creating an ambiance that felt more like a dream than reality. The bed was neatly made, with fluffy pillows and a quilt that seemed to promise comfort after a long day of anticipation. The windows were slightly ajar, letting in a breeze that brought with it the faint scent of the city — a blend of street food, fresh rain, and distant memories.*

*Pandey, ever the gentleman, immediately took on the role of caretaker. His instinct was always to put Vanya first, ensuring she was comfortable before he thought of himself. He began making the bed for her, smoothing out the creases in the sheets and fluffing the pillows, as though arranging a space of tranquility for her to rest in. His actions were calm, steady, and deliberate, a reflection of the care he held for her. When he was finished, he looked up at her, as if seeking approval for the little world he had just created for her within the four walls of the room.*

*"All set. You can take the bed," he said, standing up straight with a small, pleased smile. "I'll take the couch, of course."*

*Vanya, who had been watching him with quiet amusement, raised an eyebrow. She had anticipated this — the ever-dutiful Pandey, who would rather sleep in discomfort than impose on anyone. She chuckled to herself, knowing full well that this time, she wouldn't let him get away with it.*

*"Pandey," she said, her voice carrying a firm yet playful edge, "we're here together. You're not sleeping on that uncomfortable couch." There was no room for debate in her tone, only a quiet command. She wasn't going to let him be so self-sacrificial. This was their time, their moment to embrace each other fully — and that meant no unnecessary distance, not even in sleep.*

*Pandey paused, blinking in surprise, before breaking into a reluctant smile. "Fine," he conceded, his eyes glinting with a mischievous spark. "I'll sleep on the edge of the bed. Happy?"*

*Vanya tilted her head, sizing him up with a thoughtful expression, then pouted exaggeratedly. "That's not good enough," she teased, crossing her arms in mock disappointment. But despite her playful demeanor, there was a softness in her gaze that revealed how much she truly cared about his comfort, even in the smallest things.*

*She made her way over to the bed, slipping under the covers with a graceful ease, her body sinking into the soft mattress. As she settled in, she cast a glance at Pandey, who was still standing by the bed with*

a slightly bemused smile, his hands tucked into his pockets.
"Okay," she said, her voice quieter now, "how about you just stay.
You're not sleeping on that couch." She gestured for him to join her,
the invitation clear but unspoken. "We've got three whole days,
Pandey. Don't waste the time we have."
Pandey stood still for a moment, as if contemplating the decision.
The thought of sharing such a small, intimate space with her — a
space that was so far removed from their usual college lives — made
his heart race with both excitement and a touch of uncertainty. But
then he smiled, his usual reserve melting away in the warmth of her
presence. Slowly, he stepped forward and climbed onto the bed beside
her, settling onto the edge as promised.
Vanya didn't immediately make a move, instead watching him with
a twinkle in her eyes. She knew how important it was for him to
maintain his composure, to keep everything in balance, and she wasn't
about to rush him. But the evening was still young, and she had a
feeling that their time together was only just beginning.
As she turned to face him, her eyes bright with a secret knowledge,
Pandey glanced at her, a smile tugging at the corners of his lips. He
didn't quite understand what was happening between them, but in that
moment, he didn't need to. All he knew was that he was with her, and
that was more than enough.
Vanya, meanwhile, was already scheming — her mind filled with
playful ideas of how to make the most of these three days, of how to
make every second count. And she had a feeling that this hotel room,
with its warm lighting and simple comfort, would be the perfect setting
for whatever adventure lay ahead.

# CHAPTER THIRTY-SEVEN

# The Fall of Night

*As the evening deepened into night, Vanya's playful nature took over. She inched closer to Pandey, her every movement deliberate yet subtle. Pandey, aware of her antics, tried to maintain his composure but couldn't help stealing glances at her.*

*"What are you up to, Vanya Jain?" he asked, his voice tinged with mock suspicion.*

*"Nothing," she replied, her tone feigning innocence.*

*She continued her silent pursuit, her fingers brushing against his arm. Pandey finally gave in, pulling her close with a laugh. Their eyes met, and the room seemed to shrink around them. The world outside ceased to exist as they lost themselves in each other.*

*Vanya's lips found his, soft and eager, and the kiss deepened with every passing second. Pandey's hands traced the contours of her back, their touch igniting sparks that traveled through her body. The intensity of the moment was matched only by the tenderness with which they held each other, as though afraid to let go.*

# The Morning After

*The morning was quiet, serene, as if the world outside had slowed to match the stillness inside the room. The golden rays of sunlight, soft and gentle, poured through the curtains, casting their warmth over the room like a blanket. It was the kind of morning that seemed to stretch on forever, inviting the two of them to savor each fleeting moment.*

*Pandey woke first, his body heavy with the lingering warmth of sleep, but his heart light with something deeper, something he couldn't quite articulate yet. His gaze immediately found Vanya beside him, curled up against him with her head resting on his chest. Her soft, even breathing and the way she lay there so peacefully made his heart swell. He gently brushed a stray lock of hair from her face, marveling at how natural it felt to have her this close, to be a part of this quiet moment. The love he felt for her was overwhelming, profound—an emotion so powerful that it left him breathless. For a moment, the weight of it all seemed too much to bear, but in the most beautiful way possible.*

*Vanya stirred, the warmth of the morning sun coaxing her out of sleep. Her eyes fluttered open, slowly, lazily, adjusting to the light. When her gaze met his, it was as if the rest of the world faded away. A soft, lazy smile spread across her lips, and she whispered, barely above a breath, "Good morning, Pandey."*

*"Good morning, Vanya Jain," he replied, his voice husky from sleep, thick with the quiet intimacy of the moment. His words were soft, as though he was afraid to break the spell that held them both, afraid to speak too loudly and disturb the perfect peace between them.*

*For a while, neither of them moved. They simply lay there, the space between them filled with the warmth of their connection, the quiet hum of their hearts beating in sync. There were no words needed; they had already spoken volumes to each other, without saying a single thing. The simplicity of the moment, the ordinary and yet extraordinary feeling of being together, was a kind of magic they had both come to cherish.*

*Pandey ran his fingers through her hair absentmindedly, his touch gentle and tender. Vanya, still half-dreaming, nestled closer into his embrace, her cheek resting against his chest, her breath warm against his skin. Time seemed to slow around them, the only sounds the quiet rustle of the sheets and their gentle breaths, as if the universe itself was holding its breath for them, letting them savor this rare and precious stillness.*

*It was in these moments—the soft, unspoken ones—that they both realized how far they had come. From two people who had walked into each other's lives almost by accident, to this shared silence, this shared space where love didn't need to be declared, because it was already known. There was something so perfect in their connection, something that transcended the need for words. It was in the way they looked at each other, in the way their bodies fit together as if they had been made for this. It was the kind of love that didn't need to shout; it simply was.*

*And there, in the soft light of that morning, with the world outside still and quiet, Pandey knew this was it. This was the moment he would always remember. This was his home now, not the walls of any room or the place he had come from, but the feeling of being with her, of being seen by her, of knowing that they had built something here that no one could ever take away.*

*Vanya, her eyes half-lidded, glanced up at him, catching the quiet affection in his gaze. Without a word, she traced her fingers along the edge of his jaw, smiling at how easy it was to be with him. How natural it felt to be wrapped in his arms, to wake up to him like this, no pretenses, no barriers—just them, in this sacred space they had created together.*

*As the sun continued to rise, casting its golden light over their entwined forms, the world outside would eventually wake up, pulling them back into its demands. But for now, they were allowed to simply exist here, in this perfect moment, in this perfect peace. And in that quiet stillness, they both knew: this was love. This was home.*

# CHAPTER THIRTY-NINE

# A Day of Exploration

*The days that followed were a blur of vibrant colors and intoxicating energy, a whirlwind of passion, laughter, and discovery. They wandered the city like two curious souls, completely immersed in each other's presence, discovering not just the sights around them but also the depths of their connection. Hand in hand, they explored the narrow alleys and bustling markets, the streets alive with the hum of activity, their laughter rising above the noise like a sweet melody that only they could hear.*

*Every corner they turned seemed to hold a new adventure, and each new discovery became a cherished memory etched into the fabric of their time together. They sat on park benches, sharing a plate of spicy street food, savoring the heat and the flavors, their fingers brushing with every bite. Vanya would steal a playful glance, a mischievous smile dancing on her lips, and Pandey, unable to resist, would lean in for a kiss that was soft and sweet, stealing a moment of intimacy amidst the hustle and bustle of the city. They weren't concerned with the world around them, only with the magic they had found in each other.*

*Their visits to the museum were no less enchanting. They wandered through the halls, touching on the art that lined the walls, but their attention was always on each other. In quiet corners, far from prying eyes, they shared stolen kisses, their bodies pressing together as though they had always belonged in each other's arms. Their connection was magnetic, a force that drew them closer with every glance, every laugh, every brush of their fingertips. Even the most mundane moments felt special—simply because they were together.*

*When the sun began to set and the city turned golden, casting long shadows on the ground, they returned to their hotel. There, the world outside seemed to fade away completely. The hotel room became their sanctuary, a space where only they existed. The nights were filled with whispered confessions and stolen touches, their voices soft, the air thick with longing. In the stillness of the room, their desires would unfold, slowly and deliciously, like a secret shared only between them.*

*Vanya, always the playful tease, would inch closer to Pandey, her eyes glinting with mischief. She would challenge him, coaxing him with teasing words, knowing exactly how to keep him on his toes. Pandey, ever the quick-witted one, would match her every move, his retorts sharp but filled with affection. Their banter was a dance, a back-and-forth rhythm that felt as natural as breathing. It was in these moments, the quiet ones before the storm, that they revealed the depths of their connection—each teasing remark, each playful jab, an unspoken promise of more.*

*But beyond the jokes and playful exchanges, there was something deeper stirring between them—something electric and raw. Every touch, every glance, seemed charged with an energy that was impossible to ignore. When Pandey reached for her hand, it was like a spark had ignited between them. When she leaned in to whisper something in his ear, his breath would hitch, his pulse quickening. It wasn't just physical attraction—it was a bond that transcended the surface, a connection so intense that it left them both breathless.*

*The room, filled with the soft glow of the bedside lamp, became a world of its own, cocooning them in a bubble of passion and intimacy. They would lie together, bodies entwined, talking about everything and nothing, sharing secrets, hopes, and dreams. Sometimes, there were no words at all, just the sound of their hearts beating in sync, the steady rhythm of their love.*

*In those quiet moments, they understood something profound. It wasn't just about the playful teasing or the stolen kisses—it was the way they fit together, the way their souls intertwined in perfect harmony. It was the way their presence in each other's lives had filled the empty spaces, bringing a kind of peace that neither of them had*

*known before.*
*And so, as the days slipped by in a blur of passion and joy, they allowed themselves to savor each fleeting moment, knowing that these days, these precious days spent together, would be memories they would carry with them forever.*

# Farewell to Days

*As the three days drew to a close, the inevitability of their parting cast a shadow over their time together. At the railway station, Pandey held Vanya close, his arms wrapped around her as though to shield her from the world.*

*"I'll miss you," he said, his voice breaking.*

*"And I'll miss you more," she replied, tears glistening in her eyes. Their goodbye was bittersweet, a poignant reminder of the love that bound them and the distance that would soon separate them. But as Vanya's train pulled away, Pandey knew that their bond was unbreakable. For in each other, they had found a love that transcended time and space, a love that would endure.*

*As he walked back to his car, Pandey's heart was heavy yet full. The memories of their time together played in his mind like a cherished melody, a reminder that even in their absence, their love would remain.*

# CHAPTER FORTY-ONE

# A Month Apart: Love Across the Wires "The Call"

Vanya: "Pandey, is that you? It's been forever, The days drag on, endless, and sever. How's your tea, your mornings, your books? Do you still sit by the window, lost in your looks?"

Pandey: "Vanya, my sun, my moon's glow, Time halts without you; it ebbs so slow. My tea's warm, yet it's missing your cheer, The mornings are empty when you're not near."

Vanya: "Pandey, is that you? It's been forever, The days drag on, endless, and sever. How's your tea, your mornings, your books? Do you still sit by the window, lost in your looks?"

Pandey: "Vanya, my sun, my moon's glow, Time halts without you; it ebbs so slow. My tea's warm, yet it's missing your cheer, The mornings are empty when you're not near."

### Night's Whispers

Vanya: "Do you know, Pandey, what I miss the most? Your voice at twilight, your words like a toast. The laughter that spills in our nightly banter, The way you read poems—your voice a dancer."

Pandey: "And you, my Vanya, are my sweetest muse, Your giggles, your stories, your love-infused clues. I miss how your eyes close when you smile, These nights are so cruel, I count every mile."

*The holiday stretched, the days grew long,*
*Each hour without him felt so wrong.*
*"Pandey," she murmured, her voice a plea,*
*"These weeks apart feel like eternity."*
*"Hold on, my love," he reassured,*
*"For soon this ache will be cured."*
*They clung to hope, a fragile thread,*
*Love's fire burning, where others fled*

### *<u>The Night's Confession</u>*

*"Do you think of me in the quiet hours?"*
*Vanya's question unfurled like flowers.*
*"Always," Pandey said, "You're in my breath,*
*From morning's rise to the night's death."*
*"I wish I could hear your heartbeat now,*
*Feel its rhythm, its sacred vow.*
*This phone cannot carry the warmth I crave,*
*A love so boundless, so beautifully brave."*
*"Vanya," he sighed, "soon we'll reunite,*
*Erase this distance, end this plight.*
*Until then, my heart is yours to keep,*
*Through the days awake, and the nights asleep."*

### *<u>The Void of Touch</u>*

*"Do you miss my touch?" Pandey asked,*
*His voice a mask for emotions unmasked.*
*Vanya's silence, a pause profound,*
*Then she whispered, "Every second, it's all around."*
*"Your arms, my home, your heartbeat, my tune,*
*Without you, life's an endless monsoon.*
*Come back soon, don't make me wait,*
*Distance, this villain, I'll berate."*
*Pandey's sigh reached through the line,*
*"This void, Vanya, is a test divine.*
*But hold on, my love, just a little more,*
*Soon, our moments will begin to soar."*

### <u>A Silent Morning</u>

Vanya: "Pandey, mornings without you feel hollow. Even coffee lacks its warmth."

Pandey: "And tea without your chatter tastes bland. Tell me, what did the dawn say to you today?"

Vanya: "It asked me why I'm not smiling. And I answered, 'Because he's not here.'" Pandey: "The sun's jealous, Vanya, for even its warmth can't match the fire you spark in me."

Vanya: "What will we do when we meet again? Will you show me that bookstore in the lane? Or shall we sit by the lake with the stars above? Dreaming of futures, drowning in love."

Pandey: "First, I'll hold you, and time will cease, Your warmth in my arms, my world's only peace. Then to the bookstore, and the lake's quiet shore, Together, forever, dreaming evermore."

### <u>The Restless Nights</u>

Vanya: "Pandey, do you sleep, or do you lie awake? Does the moonlight mock the dreams it takes? I close my eyes, and your face appears, A silhouette of love, through my sleepy tears."

Pandey: "Sleep eludes me; the stars are unkind, They speak of you in whispers, in ways undefined. I'd give the world for a single embrace, To hold you close, to touch your face."

### <u>Shared Dreams</u>

Vanya: "Let's dream, Pandey, and plan something bold, Let's visit the hills where stories are told. A cabin in the woods, a fire that burns bright, Us against the world, beneath starlit nights."

Pandey: "Dreams, my love, are the threads we weave, I'll take your hand, and we'll never grieve. To the hills, to the woods, to the lakes afar, Anywhere with you is my guiding star."

### <u>The Little Things</u>

Vanya: "Do you miss the small things, my silly little acts? The way I tap your shoulder, the quirky little facts? Do you still hum the song I taught you that day? Do the sparrows remind you of our secret way?"

Pandey: "Every tap, every song, every glance of yours, Is etched in my heart, where eternity pours. The sparrows still chatter, the tune still plays, In the echoes of love, through lonesome days."

### ***The Pain of Separation***

*Vanya: "This distance, Pandey, is a test too steep, It wakes me from dreams; it shatters my sleep. How much longer till we're free from this? Till your arms hold me, till we find our bliss?"*

*Pandey: "Patience, my love, though the wait is long, Our bond is resilient, our hearts are strong. Soon the clock will bow to our demands, And I'll find my solace in your clasped hands."*

### ***Midnight Emails***

*Pandey: "Check your inbox, Vanya, before the day ends, A poem awaits you, love's messages it sends. Each line holds the weight of this month apart, Each word's a whisper, straight from my heart."*

*Vanya (reads): "'O Vanya, my dawn, my twilight's hymn, These words are a reflection of the love I brim. If distance were rivers, I'd build a bridge wide, To walk to your laughter, to stand by your side.'"*

*Vanya: "Your emails Pandey, are my midnight delight, They paint our love in colors so bright. I read them twice, then thrice again, Each line a whisper, a balm for my pain."*

*Pandey: "If words could traverse the miles between, I'd write you an ocean, a verdant green. Each email is a vessel, carrying my heart, A piece of me with you, though we're apart."*

### ***The Promise***

*Vanya: "Promise me, Pandey, when this month is done, We'll write our story beneath the setting sun. No more calls, no more screens to divide, Just you and me, walking side by side."*

*Pandey: "I promise, Vanya, as sure as the sky, This month will end, and we'll no longer sigh. Our love will dance in the realm of the real, Every moment with you, a dream I'll steal."*

### ***Planning Their Reunion***

*Vanya: "Tell me, Pandey, where shall we go? To the bookstore, the lake, or fields aglow? What shall we eat, what tales will we share? What memories shall we make, what love will we dare?"*

*Pandey: "To the bookstore, my love, for stories untold, To the lake, where waters whisper secrets of old. We'll feast on laughter, on dreams that unfold, In the embrace of love, where the heart is bold."*

### ***Goodnight, My Love***

*Vanya: "Goodnight, Pandey, though it's never enough, These calls are a lifeline, but the wait is tough. Dream of me, as I dream of you, And let the stars guide our love's rendezvous."*
*Pandey: "Goodnight, Vanya, my sweetest refrain, Your voice is the melody that soothes my pain. Till dawn breaks and we talk once more, My heart is with you, to its very core."*
*The conversations continued, each verse a testament to their love and longing. With every word spoken, with every email written, their hearts grew closer, even as the miles stretched long. And as the month passed, the anticipation of reunion burned brighter, a love story blooming like the first light of dawn.*
*Pandey's poems became her treasure,*
*Each word a token of endless pleasure.*

*"My Vanya," he wrote, "you are my dawn,*
*The light I seek when hope is gone."*
*She replied in kind, her words a balm,*
*"My Pandey, my love, my ocean calm."*
*Their correspondence a bridge of gold,*
*A testament to love's story, untold.*
*The night before her journey home,*
*They spoke until the stars were alone.*
*"Pandey," she whispered, "tomorrow is near,*
*I'll be in your arms, my love, my dear."*
*He smiled, though his heart did ache,*
*"I'll wait for you at dawn's first break."*
*They said goodnight, their souls entwined,*
*Two hearts in love, perfectly aligned.*
*That morning came, as mornings do,*
*A sky of hope, painted in blue.*
*He stood at the platform, eyes aglow,*
*Her train arriving, her face to show.*
*Their reunion, a moment pure,*
*A love so vast, no force could deter.*
*And as they embraced, the world fell away,*

*Their love eternal, come what may.*

# CHAPTER FORTY-TWO

# The Summer Serenade of Vanya and Pandey

*The summer days arrived with their golden warmth, filling the air with a soft glow that seemed to echo the deepening of Vanya and Pandey's connection. The heat of the sun mirrored the fire that burned between them, a fire that was still gentle, but growing ever stronger with each passing moment. As the world around them shifted into the carefree rhythm of summer, so too did their bond, taking on a new, more intimate form—a season of love blossoming in its purest, most tender expression.*

*The college corridors, once merely places of routine and exchange, now felt charged with an energy unique to them. Every glance they shared became a secret, a silent conversation only they understood. Pandey would pass by Vanya between classes, and for a fleeting second, their eyes would meet—no words needed—just a connection so deep it spoke louder than anything they could say. Those quiet exchanges in the halls, where the world seemed to pause around them, were their own brand of magic. It wasn't just about the proximity, but about what lay behind each look—a shared understanding, a promise held in the silence.*

*Even in the midst of bustling streets, when the heat of summer wrapped around them, they found moments of solitude in each other. The city, usually filled with noise and movement, became a backdrop to their quiet world. Pandey would often catch Vanya's hand in his as they walked, fingers intertwined as if the simple act of holding on* grounded them amidst the chaos of the outside world. Their steps were in sync, their hearts beating in rhythm, as they moved through the crowds—together but apart from it all, as if they were in their own universe, where only they existed.

Vanya's laughter became a constant melody in the soundtrack of their days. It echoed in the cafes they visited, the streets they strolled, and the quiet moments in between. Her laugh had a way of wrapping around him, light and free, as if it carried with it all the joy of the world. Pandey's responses were often softer, quieter, but no less filled with affection. He cherished every word she spoke, every chuckle that bubbled from her lips, every moment of joy she gave him. The exchange of jokes, teasing, and even the quiet pauses between them felt meaningful, like they were building a language of their own—a language that didn't need to be spoken out loud.

As their love grew, so did the tenderness with which they cared for each other. It wasn't grand gestures, but the little things that meant the most. Pandey would bring her her favorite chai between classes, and she would tease him about his overprotective nature, yet secretly adore the way he always took care of her. On days when the heat became overwhelming, Vanya would offer him her scarf or share an iced drink she'd picked up for herself, her smile a reminder of how much she wanted to look after him. Each act, no matter how small, became a testament to the love they had for each other—both the quiet affection and the growing intensity.

And in the quiet corners of the city, the moments of passion began to seep in, not just in their stolen glances but in their touch, their closeness, the way they spoke to each other. It wasn't always about grand declarations of love; sometimes, it was simply in the way their fingers would brush as they sat close to each other or how they would linger for a moment longer when parting, as though neither wanted to let go. The intimacy between them grew, slow and steady, like the petals of a flower unfolding, each layer revealing more of their hearts and souls to one another.

Vanya and Pandey were learning what it meant to truly be with someone—learning the depths of trust, the quiet strength that came *from shared vulnerability, and the joy that came from simply being together. And so, summer became their season, a time where the world outside seemed to fall away, leaving only the two of them, their love growing stronger with every day that passed, every smile, every touch. Together, they built a world that was uniquely theirs—filled with the kind of love that was quiet, sure, and infinitely deep.*

# CHAPTER FORTY-THREE

# The Begining of Summer

*Summer crept in, painting their world in hues of amber, casting a warm glow that seemed to wrap around them like a soft embrace. The mornings were gentle, stretching long into the day, the air heavy with the promise of heat. For Pandey, a natural night owl, this shift in rhythm was a departure from his usual routine. Yet, in Vanya's presence, it was a change he welcomed with open arms, for she had a way of making every morning feel like a new adventure.*

*Each day, as the sun began to rise, Vanya would slip quietly into his room, the scent of fresh tea swirling around her. She'd bring him a cup, warm and spiced, the steam rising like a breath of comfort. It wasn't just the tea that warmed him, though—it was the way she cared for him, the tenderness she brought to every simple act. It felt like more than just a gesture; it was her way of nurturing, a motherly touch intertwined with the affection of a lover.*

*"Pandey, wake up! The world won't wait for you to unravel its beauty," she would tease, her voice light and musical, laced with affection and mischief. Her words, like the morning itself, carried a promise—a promise that the day ahead would hold something wonderful, something worth waking for.*

*Pandey would smile groggily, eyes still heavy with sleep, and pull her close in a sleepy hug. His arms wrapped around her, a protective gesture that felt both tender and natural. His voice, muffled against the softness of her hair, would carry a quiet affection. "You are my world," he'd murmur, the words almost a whisper but deep with meaning.*

*Her cheeks would flush at his words, a subtle warmth spreading across her skin, mirroring the sun's ascent. There was something about his quiet affection, the simplicity of his love, that made her heart swell. It wasn't the grand declarations, but these quiet, intimate moments that held more weight than anything else. She'd smile, her laughter light and carefree, as her fingers lightly brushed the strands of his hair. "And you," she'd reply softly, "are mine."*

*In that moment, as the day stretched ahead, it was just the two of them—wrapped in the soft cocoon of morning light and warmth, where the world outside felt distant and everything else faded into the background. They were simply, undeniably, theirs.*

# College Days & Stolen Memories

*Their days at college were woven with the kind of intimacy that wasn't always obvious to the outside world but felt monumental to them. Every shared note, every playful argument, every brief touch was like a delicate thread, weaving their connection tighter, crafting a story they alone understood.*

*Vanya, ever the sharp-witted spark, would relentlessly tease Pandey during their lunch breaks, always challenging him with debates that were as much about showing off her intellect as they were about drawing him out of his shell. Their banter would fill the air, quick and witty, leaving the surrounding friends in awe of their mental sparring. No one else could quite keep up with the sharpness of their exchanges. For Vanya, these moments were her way of keeping Pandey on his toes, drawing him into the playful rhythm of their relationship, while for Pandey, it was an opportunity to see the fire in her eyes, that brilliance that made him fall for her all over again.*

*But it was the library—the quiet sanctuary of the written word—that held the most enchantment for them. It wasn't the dust-covered shelves or the whisper of pages turning that created the magic, though. It was the way they'd sit together, close enough for their shoulders to brush, yet far enough apart that no one would think they were anything more than study partners. In those moments, everything else faded away. The scent of old books, the muffled sounds of hushed conversations, the soft clicking of keyboards—they were all* background noise to the quiet electricity crackling between them. They shared earphones, the music weaving their hearts together in a melody only they could hear.

Pandey, always the more reserved one, would find it impossible not to lean in closer. His lips would hover near her ear, his voice a quiet, teasing whisper that sent shivers down her spine. **"Focus, Ms. Jain, or I might just distract you further,"** he'd say, his breath brushing her skin as he spoke. The words were playful, but the intent behind them was something deeper—a promise of more, of something that went beyond the confines of books and classrooms.

Vanya would smile, that mischievous grin tugging at her lips, but she never fully resisted. She'd pretend to push him away, her heart racing, even as she knew that, in truth, the only thing distracting her was the proximity of his presence. They were both caught in the magic of the moment, pretending to study but letting their hearts do the talking, each glance and touch a silent confession of the bond they were building, one small moment at a time.

In the library, amid the quiet rustle of pages, their connection wasn't about words or grand gestures—it was the shared space between them, the unspoken understanding, the thrill of being together despite the world around them. It was here, in the hushed stillness, that they both felt the most alive.

# CHAPTER FORTY-FIVE

# The Summer's Kiss

*One evening, as the sun dipped low, casting a warm golden glow across the college garden, the world around them seemed to stand still. The campus, usually alive with the hum of voices and footsteps, was quiet, almost as if nature itself was holding its breath. The air was thick with the scent of jasmine and the faint rustling of leaves.*

*Vanya, clad in a light summer dress that swayed with the breeze, walked beside Pandey, her laughter ringing out like music. He had just told one of his typically lame jokes, but Vanya's infectious laughter made it sound like the funniest thing in the world. The sound of it lingered in the evening air, wrapping them in a cocoon of happiness.*

*Pandey, always the quiet observer, watched her with a smile that mirrored her joy. He took a step closer, his voice lowering, as if the moment was too fragile to disturb with anything loud. "Vanya, do you know what makes the sun jealous every day?"*

*Vanya raised an eyebrow, her curiosity piqued. She slowed her pace, turning to face him fully, her eyes sparkling in the soft evening light. "What?" she asked, her voice teasing yet expectant, knowing Pandey always had a clever response up his sleeve.*

*Without missing a beat, Pandey's gaze softened, and he closed the distance between them, his presence enveloping her. "You," he said simply, his voice smooth, a gentle whisper meant only for her.*

*A stunned silence followed. Vanya blinked, caught off guard by the sincerity in his words. Her heart skipped a beat, her pulse quickening as she registered the look in his eyes—the raw honesty and affection that made her breath catch in her throat. For a moment, the world seemed to disappear, leaving only the two of them standing in the glow of the fading sunlight.*

*Pandey's hands, steady but tender, reached up to cup her face. The warmth of his touch sent a shiver down her spine. Her breath hitched as his thumb gently traced the outline of her cheek. And then, without another word, their lips met.*

*The kiss was soft at first, a slow exploration, as if both of them were savoring the moment they had unknowingly been waiting for. But as the seconds passed, their connection deepened, the kiss growing more intense, more urgent, as though the kiss itself was a declaration of the emotions that had quietly been building between them. There was a spark, an electricity that coursed through their veins, as though the entire world had shifted to align in that perfect moment.*

*Vanya's hands found their way to his shoulders, gripping him as if to steady herself in the face of such raw emotion. Pandey's arms tightened around her, pulling her closer, as if he couldn't bear the distance between them any longer. Everything they had felt, all the words they had never said, found their voice in that kiss.*

*It was a kiss that spoke of more than just affection—it spoke of promises and unspoken dreams, of years spent building a bond that had quietly but surely blossomed into something beautiful. Their hearts beat in tandem, echoing the quiet rhythm of the evening as they lost themselves in each other.*

*And when they finally broke apart, their foreheads touched, breaths coming in shallow gasps, they shared a smile—one that was all-encompassing, all-knowing. The world around them seemed to settle back into its rhythm, but for Pandey and Vanya, everything had changed in that brief but unforgettable moment. The garden, the fading sunlight, their shared laughter—it was all part of a moment they would carry with them forever.*

# Nights of Intamacy

*The nights were theirs, a sanctuary from the outside world, where time seemed to slow and the chaos of the day dissolved into the quiet comfort of Pandey's small apartment. The simplicity of those moments became their refuge—a space where they could just be, away from the demands of the world.*

*Vanya often took charge of dinner, her love for Pandey showing through every dish she prepared. "You're spoiling me," Pandey would tease as he tasted the curry, the warm spices filling his senses and wrapping him in the comfort of home.*

*"And you deserve it," Vanya would reply, her voice soft but firm as she planted a quick kiss on his cheek before returning to the kitchen. She worked with quiet precision, moving around the small apartment, the soft clinking of pots and pans the only sound, except for the occasional laughter that bubbled up between them.*

*After dinner, they would retreat to the couch, a familiar spot that had seen their shared joys, quiet talks, and tender silences. Their legs would tangle together as they settled into the cushions, each moment stretching into the next. The lamp beside them cast a warm glow, illuminating their faces, painting the space with a golden hue that matched the soft intimacy of the evening. The world outside was forgotten—here, it was just the two of them.*

*They'd talk about everything and nothing—sharing dreams about the future, laughing over the small, silly things that only they understood. Pandey would sometimes pull out his journal, reading aloud poetry he had written for her. His words were like a spell, wrapping around her heart and soul, each verse an expression of the love he felt but couldn't always express in normal conversation. The rhythm of his voice, the cadence of his words, and the sincerity in his eyes made her feel as though she was hearing his soul speak.*

*Vanya would be mesmerized by his voice, her heart swelling with affection. Sometimes, in the middle of a poem, she would lean in, pulling him into a kiss so passionate it would leave them breathless. The kiss would linger, soft and sweet at first, then grow deeper, each one drawing them closer, until the rest of the world no longer existed. Their hearts beat together in the quiet, tender rhythm of their love.*

*But one night, something shifted. Their kisses grew more urgent, more filled with a need they had only just begun to acknowledge. Vanya's hands roamed across Pandey's chest, feeling the warmth of his skin beneath the fabric of his shirt. Her breath quickened as his fingers traced the familiar path along her back, sending waves of warmth through her body. The soft cotton of her kurta brushed against him, the fabric a mere whisper of the closeness they shared.*

*She shivered, but not from the chill of the evening air—no, it was the warmth of his touch, the electricity of their connection, that made her pulse race. Their hands explored, not just the surface of each other's bodies but the very essence of their love. Each touch, each caress, was an unspoken conversation—a language that transcended words. In that moment, nothing else mattered but the way their bodies and hearts intertwined, syncing to the rhythm of their shared love.*

*Pandey's lips found her neck, pressing gentle kisses against her skin, his breath hot against her. Vanya let out a soft sigh, her hands threading through his hair as she pulled him closer, her chest rising and falling with each breath. The world outside continued to spin, but in that apartment, beneath the soft light of the lamp, they existed in their own space, where love was quiet, yet loud in its intensity. The language of their hearts was spoken without words, only through the gentle touch of hands, the soft press of lips, and the warmth that radiated from them both.*

*In those moments, they were no longer two people—they were one. A shared soul, bound by a love so deep, so undeniable, that nothing in the world could ever come close to comparing.*

# Arguments & Apologies

*Their love, while tender, was not without its storms. A silly disagreement over plans for the weekend turned into an argument one afternoon.*

*"Why can't you just listen, Pandey? I'm trying to make things special for us!" Vanya exclaimed, her eyes glistening with unshed tears.*

*"And I just want to spend time with you, without all this planning," Pandey retorted, his voice rising.*

*The silence that followed was unbearable, but Pandey, unable to see her upset, pulled her into a hug. "I'm sorry," he whispered. "You're right. I'm just an idiot."*

*Vanya, melting in his embrace, chuckled through her tears. "You are an idiot, but you're my idiot."*

# CHAPTER FORTY-EIGHT

# Summer of Sensual Nights

*The night after their argument hung heavy with the weight of unspoken words, but the silence between them was no longer filled with tension. Instead, it carried a quiet intimacy, a mutual understanding that no fight could break the bond they shared. In the dim light of the room, they lay together, their bodies entwined as though they were meant to fit this way, like two pieces of a puzzle that had found their perfect match.*

*Vanya's fingers slowly traced through Pandey's hair, the gesture soft and comforting. It was a silent apology, a way of showing him that despite the words spoken earlier, she still held him close, still wanted him near. Pandey's thumb gently ran along the outline of her lips, his touch tender as though savoring the very essence of her.*

*The quiet of the night was punctuated only by their shared breaths, the rise and fall of their chests in perfect synchrony. Pandey's voice broke the silence, husky and low as he whispered, "You're everything I've ever wanted."*

*Vanya's heart swelled at his words, a rush of warmth flooding her chest. She leaned in, her lips brushing against his as she replied in the same hushed tone, "And you, Pandey, are my chaos and calm." Her words were simple but heavy with meaning, a recognition of how he brought both storm and peace into her life, and how she wouldn't have it any other way.*

*The tension of the argument faded as their lips met again, this time deeper, more desperate, each kiss a promise of forgiveness, of understanding, of the unconditional love they had for each other. Their bodies seemed to find their rhythm once more, an unspoken connection that surpassed any disagreement. It was a reassurance, an affirmation that despite the bumps in the road, their love was unwavering, that no matter how chaotic their lives might become, they would always return to each other.*

*The summer breeze flowed through the open window, its cool touch a contrast to the heat that rose between them. The air was thick with the scent of night blooming flowers, and the soft rustling of leaves outside added to the stillness in the room. Yet, within the walls of their shared space, everything felt alive, every touch, every sigh, every heartbeat.*

*They didn't need words anymore. Their bodies, their hearts, spoke the language of love, unbroken and unyielding. Their union, their coming together, was not just physical—it was a meeting of souls, a deep connection that transcended the limitations of speech. In each other's arms, they found peace, solace, and the unwavering certainty that their love was the one constant in a world that constantly shifted around them.*

*As the night stretched on, they lay in the comfort of each other's embrace, the outside world forgotten. Time seemed to slow, and the weight of the day—the argument, the tension—melted away with every kiss, every touch. They had come through it stronger, their love tested but unbroken, ready to face whatever came next. And as the summer breeze whispered through the window, carrying with it the promise of new beginnings, they knew they had each other. And that was enough.*

# CHAPTER FORTY-NINE

# Plans for Tomorrow

*As the long summer days drifted into golden afternoons, Vanya and Pandey found themselves in a comfortable rhythm, anticipating the future while savoring the present. Their days were a blend of late-night talks, shared meals, and quiet moments, each one weaving them closer together. But in the midst of their familiar routine, they began to envision what the next chapter of their story would look like.*

*It was during one of their frequent chai sessions, nestled in the corner of their favorite café, when the idea first emerged. The sun cast a warm glow through the window, and the steam rising from their cups seemed to mirror the daydreams brewing in Vanya's mind. She set down her cup, her fingers lingering on the porcelain, and looked up at Pandey with a gleam of excitement in her eyes.*

*"We should go on a road trip," she said, her voice laced with anticipation.*

*Pandey raised an eyebrow, intrigued by the suggestion. "A road trip?" he echoed, setting his own cup aside and giving her his full attention. "Where to?"*

*Vanya leaned back in her chair, her thoughts racing with possibilities. The world was vast, and there were so many places she wanted to see, but she knew it wasn't the destination that mattered—it was the journey. It was the thought of being with Pandey, of exploring new horizons together, that made her heart race. She smiled, her mind drifting to the roads they could take, the towns they could visit, the moments they could create.*

"*Anywhere,*" *she replied with a shrug, her eyes shining with mischief. "Somewhere we can be free. Just the two of us."*

*Pandey's lips curled into a soft smile as he watched her, the excitement in her voice infectious. He knew that whatever their adventure entailed, it would be perfect because it was with her. The idea of taking a road trip with Vanya—her laughter filling the car, her hand in his as they drove through the open roads—was enough to send a thrill through his veins.*

**"Anywhere you want, Ms. Jain,"** *he said, his gaze never leaving hers.* **"As long as you're by my side."**

*The simplicity of his words wrapped around her heart like a warm blanket, and she leaned across the table, her hand brushing his. In that moment, they didn't need anything else. The world outside seemed to fade away, leaving just the two of them and the unspoken promise of adventures to come.*

*Their plans were made on the spot, as natural and easy as breathing. They'd spend the rest of the summer making lists, picking out places they both wanted to see, and imagining the long drives ahead, with music playing softly in the background and the open road stretching out before them.*

*As the sun began to set, casting a fiery glow over the horizon, they sat there for a while longer, content in the quiet knowledge that this road trip—this adventure—was just another chapter in the story they were writing together, one filled with love, laughter, and the kind of intimacy that only deepens with time.*

# A Touch

*Vanya's care for Pandey was a quiet, steady force that held them both in a delicate balance. It wasn't just the small gestures—though they were endless—that spoke volumes about her affection. It was the way she saw him, with a tenderness that felt almost maternal, yet deeply romantic. She understood his habits, the way he'd skip meals in favor of work or get lost in a book until the world outside faded into oblivion. And it was in these moments that she would become the anchor he so desperately needed, guiding him back to the present with a plate of food or a cup of tea.*

*"You'll ruin your health if you keep skipping meals," she'd scold, her brow furrowed in concern as she placed the food in front of him. Her voice, though gentle, carried the weight of love—love that sought not to control, but to protect, to nurture, to keep him from slipping away into the depths of his own thoughts.*

*He'd look at her, his heart swelling with affection, always marveling at how much she seemed to care. "And you'll ruin me with all this love," he'd tease, his arms wrapping around her in a quick hug, as if to say "thank you" without words.*

*Vanya, always with a soft chuckle, would pull away just enough to meet his gaze, her eyes a reflection of both mischief and tenderness. She didn't just love him; she understood him in a way no one else ever could. The way she seemed to read his soul with a single glance was something that went beyond affection—it was a deep, profound connection that transcended even the most romantic of gestures.*

*Their bond, like the weave of a timeless fabric, was composed of threads both light and heavy. Friendship was the foundation—built on years of shared moments and laughter. Romance was the color that painted their days, vivid and full of life. But it was the deep, unspoken love between them—the kind that didn't require grand gestures to be felt—that held it all together. It was a love so quiet yet so powerful, it didn't need to be explained; it simply was. It existed in the way Pandey's heart would skip a beat when Vanya smiled, in the warmth of her touch when she'd brush a strand of hair from his face, in the way her laughter felt like the most comforting melody to his ears.*

*There was a certain beauty in the simplicity of their love. It wasn't flashy, nor did it demand attention. It was, instead, a quiet force—a soft breeze that flowed between them, carrying with it the weight of everything they had yet to say, everything they had already shared. Their love was neither perfect nor easy, but it was real, and it was theirs.*

*In the moments when Vanya would scold him playfully for his lack of self-care, or when she'd lean into him, comforting him after a long day, Pandey would feel as if time stood still. In those little moments, the world outside didn't matter. All that mattered was the warmth of her presence, the steady rhythm of their hearts beating in unison. For them, love was not an ideal to be chased or a story to be written—it was something lived, something felt in the quiet exchanges and in the shared spaces between words. It was found in the simplicity of just being together, without pretense or expectation.*

*And as they moved through their days, side by side, they discovered that perhaps the deepest form of love wasn't in the grand declarations or the passionate moments. It was in the quiet understanding, the unspoken promises, and the way their lives, intertwined so seamlessly, spoke to the depth of their connection.*

# CHAPTER FIFTY-ONE

# One Year, One World

*It had been one year—a year that felt like the blink of an eye and yet an eternity, all at once. A year that existed not in hours or days, but in stolen glances, in the warmth of unspoken words, in the silent conversations that passed between them in the spaces where no sound was needed. For Pandey, Vanya was not just his love; she was the very pulse of his existence, the rhythm that guided his heart, the muse that breathed life into his thoughts.*

*She was the air he breathed and the ink he bled onto paper. A poet by soul, Pandey found himself unable to escape the pull of her essence. She had become a part of him in ways he could not articulate. It wasn't just her smile that filled his world with light; it was the way her presence could transform an ordinary moment into something extraordinary. Every time their fingers brushed or their eyes met, it felt like the universe was composing a symphony just for them.*

*He had always been a poet, but it was Vanya who had unlocked the depths of his creativity, pulling words from places he never knew existed. He found himself crafting verses in her name, her laughter echoing in every stanza, her eyes woven into every metaphor, every rhyme. She was the muse who guided his pen, the spark that ignited his deepest, most intimate thoughts. It was as though, with every line, he was trying to capture her essence, preserve it, and weave it into the fabric of time.*

*He wrote of the way her hair glinted in the sunlight, as if strands of midnight were woven into the gold of dawn. He wrote of her laughter, which was a melody that could soften the hardest of hearts and make the world seem brighter. He wrote of the way she moved through the world—graceful, confident, and untouchable, yet somehow, she had made him feel as though he belonged at her side, as though he could stand beside her and be a part of her world.*

*But it wasn't just the grand gestures of love he wrote about; it was the small, quiet moments, too. The way she would tuck her hair behind her ear when she was concentrating, the way her hand would rest gently on his when she was content, the way she would look at him as though he were the only person in the room. These were the moments that filled his heart with more love than any grand confession could, and they were the moments he tried, in vain, to capture with his words.*

*"Vanya," he would often say to her, after a moment of quiet contemplation, his voice soft, "You are the poem I never knew I needed to write. You are the verse that completes me."*

*Her eyes would soften, and a gentle smile would tug at her lips, as though she understood that he wasn't just speaking words; he was sharing the very core of his heart. And in that smile, in that simple, knowing exchange, he found the truth of his feelings—how she was not just a muse but the very heart of his creativity, the reason his soul longed to create.*

*In this year together, in the quiet unfolding of their love, Pandey had discovered something far more profound than any poetry he could write. He had found that love, in its purest form, was not something to be captured in verses or songs, but something to be lived in the small moments, the shared glances, and the gentle touches that spoke of a bond far deeper than words could convey. And as the year stretched on, with each passing day, he knew that their love would continue to fill the pages of his life, one verse at a time, forever written in the ink of his heart.*

# CHAPTER FIFTY-TWO

# The Poet & His Muse

*In the quiet of the night, Pandey sat by the window, the city's distant hum barely reaching his ears. The moon hung low in the sky, casting its soft, silvery glow across the room. The notebook, worn and well-loved, rested on his knee, its pages filled with scribbled thoughts and unfinished verses. His pen moved with a quiet urgency, tracing the words that had been circling in his mind for days, words that had grown heavy with the weight of a year's worth of love.*

*He wrote not for an audience, but for her—for Vanya. Every stroke of the pen felt like a promise, every line a whisper only she could hear. His words carried the essence of their time together, the joy, the laughter, the quiet moments of understanding, and even the quiet battles they'd fought and overcome. In his words, he wove the memories of their love, of the way she'd held his hand in silence, of the way her smile could light up the darkest of rooms.*

*"You are the fire in my veins," he wrote, the ink flowing easily, as if the words had always been waiting for the moment to be spoken. "The calm that quiets my chaos, a storm I gladly surrender to."*

*Each phrase was a piece of his soul, offered to her in the way he knew best. There were no grand speeches, no grand gestures—only the quiet, steady rhythm of a love that had built itself over time, in stolen glances, in quiet conversations, in the way they had come to understand each other without saying a word.*

*He paused for a moment, his pen hovering above the page. A small smile tugged at the corner of his lips as he thought about Vanya. She had a way of teasing him, always calling him her "Bollywood bard,"* mocking his tendency to speak in dramatic, poetic terms. She'd laugh, rolling her eyes with affection as she playfully complained about his over-the-top declarations of love.

"You're such a drama king," she'd say, grinning. "Do you have to make everything sound like a movie?"

But even as she teased him, he knew she treasured every word. She would deny it, of course, but the way her eyes softened when she read his poetry, the way she would often pull him into a quiet hug afterward, spoke louder than any words could. To her, his poetry was not just a performance—it was an intimate gift, a window into his heart that she could peer into and find the very depths of his affection for her.

It wasn't just the words themselves that mattered; it was the feeling behind them, the vulnerability with which he offered his love. Each poem was an extension of his soul, laid bare for her to see, to feel, to hold. And in return, she gave him her own quiet form of love, the way she would listen to him with rapt attention, the way her fingers would gently trace the words on the page, as though she were absorbing every sentiment, every syllable.

Pandey continued to write, the words flowing effortlessly now, as if the very act of writing was an extension of their connection, a dance of hearts and minds that no one could interrupt. He didn't need to explain his feelings for her—he simply showed them, one verse at a time. The moonlight cast its glow on the page, as though the universe itself had paused to witness this quiet act of devotion.

As he finished the poem, he leaned back against the window, a sense of peace settling over him. He knew that this—these words, this love—was something that couldn't be taken away, something that would live on in the quiet moments of their lives, in the whispered confessions and the laughter shared between them.

He folded the page carefully and tucked it into the envelope, a small but significant gesture. He didn't need to wait for the right moment to give it to her. He knew, deep down, that Vanya understood. She always did

# CHAPTER FIFTY-THREE

# Vanya, The Enigma

*Vanya Jain was an enigma, a woman who defied every definition. She was a mystery wrapped in contradictions, a whirlwind of complexities that no one, not even Pandey, could fully unravel. She could be as fierce as a storm, a force of nature that demanded attention and respect. Her laughter could fill a room with a warmth that contrasted sharply with the sharpness in her words when she was frustrated or passionate about something. Yet, beneath that intensity, there was an undeniable tenderness that she reserved for the few she truly cared for, and for Pandey, it was like a secret she let him in on, a treasure she shared with no one else.*

*She nurtured him, her love a soft but unyielding force that wrapped around him like a warm embrace, her caring gestures constant and never expected. She'd make him tea when he was sick, ensure he was eating well even when he was too caught up in his own world, and give him advice that balanced practicality and compassion. Her love for him was not a grand display but a quiet presence, always there, always unwavering. She was the kind of woman who could make even the most mundane moments feel like something special—whether it was a lazy Sunday morning spent curled up together with books, or a brief walk after class, holding hands and stealing glances at each other.*

*Yet, alongside that softness, there was a fire within her, one that could ignite at any moment. She didn't just exist in the world; she took it by storm. Her opinions were strong, her desires even stronger, and she would challenge anyone who crossed her path. She was relentless in her pursuits, especially when it came to what she believed in, and* she expected nothing less from the people she loved. With Pandey, it was a constant dance of push and pull, of challenging each other in ways that neither had ever experienced before. She questioned his beliefs, pushed him to grow beyond his comfort zone, and in doing so, taught him what it meant to evolve.

And yet, in her fierce independence, there was also a deep need for connection, a quiet vulnerability that she revealed only to him. She didn't need to be strong all the time; sometimes, it was Pandey's shoulder she leaned on when the world grew too heavy. There were nights when she would sit in silence beside him, letting his presence be the comfort she needed, a reassurance that in their chaos, there was still a balance, a quiet peace. Her love was a blend of gentle care and fiery passion, a paradox that left Pandey both grounded and elevated.

"She's my paradox," Pandey had once told a close friend, his voice thick with emotion, as though the weight of his love for her was more than he could articulate in simple words. "She's chaos and calm, light and shadow. She makes me want to be better, yet she loves me just as I am."

It was this duality that captivated him, that kept him endlessly fascinated. How could someone be so tender and yet so fierce? So free yet so loyal? Vanya was the one who could make him laugh with a single look, yet challenge him in ways no one else could. She was the fire that sparked his creativity, the anchor that held him steady when everything else felt uncertain. And as much as he loved her, he found himself in awe of her—of how she was both a force to be reckoned with and a sanctuary to return to, a woman who defied expectations, who made no apologies for the way she was.

Pandey knew that his life, his heart, would never be the same. With Vanya, he had learned that love wasn't about finding someone to complete you, but rather about finding someone who made you feel whole in your own skin. She was his mirror, his muse, his madness and peace. She was everything he never knew he needed and everything he could never imagine living without. And in her presence, Pandey had found his home, his place of peace amidst the storm of life.

# CHAPTER FIFTY-FOUR

# The Year in Moments

*Their first year together was a tapestry of memories—woven with late-night calls, stolen kisses, and quiet moments that needed no words. Time seemed to slow when they were together, as if the universe conspired to create spaces for them to simply exist in each other's presence. They had laughed until their sides ached, shared inside jokes that only the two of them could understand, and argued over the silliest of things, always knowing that these small spats only made their bond stronger. Every argument ended with a smile, a kiss, and an unspoken promise that no disagreement would ever drive them apart.*

*It was the quiet moments that held the most meaning for them, though. The way Pandey would hold her hand when they sat in silence, their fingers entwined like threads in a bond they couldn't break. How Vanya would rest her head on his shoulder, content with nothing but the rhythm of his heartbeat and the peace of knowing that, no matter what, they were there for each other.*

*But one memory stood out among all the rest—an impromptu road trip during the winter break, when the world was draped in a blanket of snow, and they found themselves driving through the countryside with no particular destination in mind. It had all started on a whim.*

*Vanya, ever the adventurous spirit, had thrown out the idea of a spontaneous getaway, and Pandey, who had always been the more cautious one, had hesitated for only a moment before agreeing.*

*They rented a car, threw some clothes in the backseat, and set off, leaving behind the mundane stresses of their everyday lives. Vanya insisted on driving, her confidence behind the wheel a stark contrast to*

*Pandey's usual careful, methodical approach. She was a force of nature in that car, her hair whipping in the wind, her laugh echoing in the open air as she sang along to the radio with reckless abandon.*

*Pandey watched her from the passenger seat, completely mesmerized by the way she lit up the world around her. The way her eyes sparkled with mischief as she drove through the winding roads, the way she seemed to lose herself in the music, not caring about anything or anyone else. To him, she was the most beautiful thing in that moment—the embodiment of freedom and joy.*

*"Keep your eyes on the road!" she had chided, laughing as she swerved slightly to avoid a pothole.*

*He couldn't help but grin, his gaze still fixed on her. "How can I when my world is sitting right here?" he had replied, his voice full of sincerity, yet laced with humor.*

*Vanya rolled her eyes, though the smile on her lips betrayed her amusement. "You're impossible," she said, playfully slapping him on the arm as he leaned in for a kiss.*

*Their laughter had filled the car, echoing into the winter night as they drove through deserted streets, the city lights fading behind them. There was no agenda, no rush to get anywhere. Just the open road, the warmth of each other's company, and the knowledge that this moment—this fleeting yet perfect moment—belonged to only them.*

*As they drove into the night, the world outside seemed to disappear, leaving them in their own little bubble. They sang along to their favorite songs, shared stories, and exchanged playful banter, all while the stars overhead glittered like a thousand little secrets waiting to be discovered. For those few days, it was as if the universe had pressed pause on the rest of their lives, allowing them to just be.*

*Vanya's hand would rest on the gearshift, occasionally brushing against his, and each time, he would feel the jolt of electricity between them, a reminder that no matter how many miles they traveled or how many years passed, they would always find their way back to each other. Pandey had never been the spontaneous type, but in that moment, with Vanya beside him, he felt free. It was as if she had unlocked a part of him he never knew existed, a part that was always craving adventure, love, and the simple joy of living in the now. It was a moment that would stay with him forever, etched into his memory like the lyrics of a song you never forget. A road trip, an unexpected adventure, and a love that had only just begun to bloom in all its wild, beautiful, and unpredictable glory.*

# CHAPTER FIFTY-FIVE

# The Sensual Bond

*Their intimacy was a dance of fire and rain—a blend of passion and tenderness that seemed to flow between them naturally, like two forces of nature colliding and creating something timeless. Pandey often marveled at the way Vanya could ignite every nerve in his body with a single touch, a simple graze of her fingers across his skin. She didn't need to speak for him to feel her presence; it was in the way her eyes met his, filled with an intensity that left him breathless, as though she could see straight through to his soul and hold it in her hands.*

*He had never known a love like this before—a love that had the power to burn him alive one moment and then soothe him like a gentle rain the next. With Vanya, he had found both the storm and the calm, both the fire that kept him alive and the rain that kept him grounded.*

*It was a balance he never thought possible, but with her, it made perfect sense. Every touch, every kiss was a promise, a delicate whisper of all that they were to each other.*

*On the night of their anniversary, the air was thick with a special kind of anticipation. The room was bathed in the soft glow of candles, their flickering light casting shadows that seemed to dance along the walls, mirroring the rhythm of their hearts. It was a quiet evening, the world outside fading into the background as they found themselves wrapped in each other's presence. There was no rush, no expectations—just the sacred space they had created together.*

*Vanya, always the one to initiate the most intimate moments, approached him slowly, her every movement deliberate, as if she was savoring the time they had. She reached out, her fingertips brushing* against Pandey's jawline, sending a wave of warmth through him. He closed his eyes for a moment, letting himself soak in the sensation of her touch—the soft pressure, the intimacy in the gesture, the way she could make him feel like he was the only person in the world that mattered.

"You're mine," she whispered, her voice low and laced with something both vulnerable and certain. There was an underlying strength in her words, a quiet power that made his heart skip a beat. She didn't need to explain it—he understood. In that moment, he knew that she had claimed him just as much as he had claimed her.

Her words hung in the air, heavy and beautiful, and for a long moment, Pandey couldn't find his voice. All he could do was gaze at her, his eyes filled with a love that could never truly be captured in words. Finally, he spoke, his voice hushed but full of certainty.

"Always."

The single word carried everything—the depth of his love, the quiet strength of his commitment, and the eternity he saw in their future together. Without another thought, he pulled her closer, capturing her lips in a kiss that was both soft and fiery. It was a kiss that spoke of forever, of all the days that had led them here and all the moments that were yet to come.

As their lips parted, they held each other close, not needing to say anything more. The world outside may have continued on with its chaos, but for them, time had stopped. They were together, and that was all that mattered.

# CHAPTER FIFTY-SIX

# Letters of Love

*Pandey's poetry, though often scrawled in his beloved notebook, had a way of spilling into other aspects of his life, most notably through emails to Vanya. Each time he wrote to her, he poured his soul into every sentence, his words flowing like a river—deep, intense, and endless. He knew she would read them slowly, savoring each word, just as he savored every moment they spent apart, eager for the day they would be reunited.*

*He would sit at his desk, the soft light of his computer screen illuminating his face as he crafted each message to her with care, knowing that his words could transcend the distance between them, if only for a brief moment.*

*__"Dearest Vanya,"__ he would begin, each letter carrying a sense of intimacy, as if he were speaking directly to her heart. "You are my chaos and my calm, the rhythm in my heartbeat, the silence in my storm. I count the days until we meet again, for every second without you is an eternity too long."*

*As the words fell from his fingers, they were not just an expression of longing; they were a declaration of everything she had come to mean to him. In those words, he found peace amidst the chaos of their busy lives. She was the anchor that kept him grounded, the melody that soothed his restless soul. To be away from her felt like being adrift on a vast, empty sea.*

*Vanya, on the other hand, would lie in her bed at night, her phone in hand, reading his words with a smile playing at her lips. She'd read each email more than once, her heart swelling with the tenderness that emanated from every line. It was as if his poetry wrapped around her like a warm blanket, bringing comfort and warmth in the midst of their separation.*

*But when it was her turn to reply, she always kept it simple, her words profound in their sincerity. "I love you more than words can say, Pandey. Come back to me soon." It was enough. The simplicity of her response reflected the depth of her love for him, a love that didn't need to be embellished. Every syllable spoke volumes, each letter a promise to be there, waiting for him, always.*

*Pandey would read her messages late at night, a soft smile curling on his lips as he imagined her voice, the way she would say those words with such affection, her eyes sparkling. And though they were miles apart, their hearts were entwined in a way that no distance could break. These letters, these small exchanges, became their little world—one where love transcended time and space, where their bond grew stronger with every word written, every message sent.*

# The Future

*As the warmth of summer began to wrap its golden arms around them, Pandey and Vanya found themselves immersed in daydreams, their conversations painted with the hues of possibilities. The air was rich with promise, and in their shared silences and laughter, they began to craft their vision of the future.*

*One evening, as they sat in their favorite café, sipping chai under the soft glow of the streetlights, Vanya let out a contented sigh. "I want to see the mountains with you," she said, her voice soft yet determined.*

*Her eyes, always so full of life, were now alight with the spark of adventure. "Let's go somewhere no one knows us, somewhere we can get lost in the beauty of it all." Her words hung in the air, creating a sense of quiet anticipation.*

*Pandey, always one to encourage her wild ideas, nodded without hesitation. "And write poetry about it," he added with a grin, his mind already envisioning the mountain landscapes, the snow-capped peaks standing tall against the sky. "We'll write about how the wind whispers secrets, how the sun kisses the earth, how your laughter will echo in the valleys." He was already picturing the mountains in his mind, and more than that, he was imagining her beside him, her voice blending with the rustling of the trees and the distant call of the birds.*

*The thought of exploring the world together, far from the confines of their college campus, filled them with an overwhelming sense of freedom. They weren't just dreaming of distant places; they were imagining a life where they could experience everything—both the mundane and the extraordinary—together. It wasn't just about the mountains or the landscapes; it was about the shared moments, the intimacy of experiencing the world as a duo, and capturing the essence of it all in poetry and memory.*

*As their conversation shifted to the next semester, their dreams began to take a more grounded form. They both had ambitions, paths to follow, but their commitment to one another never wavered. Vanya talked about her desire to excel in her field, to pursue her passion with all the vigor she had. Pandey, in turn, expressed his own aspirations, to delve deeper into his studies and to grow as a writer.*

*But through it all, they promised to support each other in every endeavor. "Whatever comes next, we'll face it together," Pandey said, his voice steady and sure. "Whether it's success or failure, we're in this side by side." His words were a pledge, not just for the next semester, but for the rest of their lives.*

*Vanya smiled, her heart swelling with affection. "We'll cheer each other on, no matter what," she agreed, her gaze softening as she reached across the table to take his hand.*

*Their love was no longer just a series of fleeting moments; it was a quiet, steady force that anchored them both, providing strength and stability as they ventured forward. As the summer breeze swirled around them, they knew that whatever the future held, they would face it together—one chai, one road trip, and one adventure at a time.*

# CHAPTER FIFTY-EIGHT

# A Love That Endures

*Their love wasn't perfect, but it was real—a beautiful, imperfect dance of highs and lows, laughter and tears. They argued, as any couple would, but each disagreement was followed by an understanding that deepened their connection. Teasing was their language, a playful way to express their affection, yet even in moments of lighthearted sarcasm, there was always an undercurrent of care. They comforted each other when the world felt too heavy, offering a refuge in the arms of one another, a place where the chaos of life seemed to fade away.*

*Through it all, they learned that love wasn't about perfection; it was about acceptance, compromise, and an unwavering commitment to stay by each other's side. Their bond was built on trust, understanding, and the quiet moments that spoke louder than words. And despite the bumps in the road, they found solace in the certainty that no matter what, they were each other's constant.*

*One evening, as the sun dipped low, casting a golden glow over the world, Pandey found himself looking at Vanya with a tenderness that spoke volumes. The warmth of the day lingered in the air, but it was the warmth between them that truly mattered. He gazed at her with a mix of awe and quiet reverence, his heart full of gratitude.*

*"You make everything worth it, you know that?" he said, his voice soft, as if he was sharing a secret meant only for her. His eyes searched hers, finding there the same depth of affection, the same quiet understanding.*

*Vanya smiled, a smile that reached her eyes, and squeezed his hand. "And you," she replied, her voice steady yet full of emotion, "make me feel like I'm home." Her words were simple, but they carried with them the weight of everything she felt—the comfort, the safety, the belonging she found in him. With him, she wasn't just herself; she was the truest version of herself. He was her anchor, her refuge, the place she returned to when the world became too much to bear.*

*Pandey's heart swelled at her words, and for a moment, the world seemed to stop. The sounds of the evening faded, leaving just the two of them in a bubble of shared understanding and love. He leaned in, pressing his forehead gently against hers, a silent promise passing between them.*

*They didn't need perfection. They had each other, and that was more than enough. In the quiet simplicity of their love, they had found a home—a home in each other's hearts, where everything was worth it, and every moment together felt like the most beautiful place to be.*

# The Twist of Tales: A Poetic Journey of Silent Love

*The campus buzzed with the excitement of youth, its vibrant energy spilling into every corner. Laughter echoed through the cafeteria as friends caught up over shared meals, while the rhythmic sound of badminton rackets striking shuttlecocks carried from the sports complex. Even in the quiet corners of the library, the murmur of students flipping through textbooks and typing out notes added to the symphony of college life. Yet, amid all this noise, two figures stood out, almost imperceptibly so. Not because they sought attention, but because of the subtle yet undeniable aura that surrounded them. Pandey and Vanya were a pair bound by something more profound than mere friendship or casual affection. Their bond was neither defined by the fleeting labels often used to categorize relationships nor limited by the traditional expectations of romance. It existed somewhere between the realms of companionship and something deeper, a territory where emotions were felt but never quite named. A situation-ship, as some would call it, that was never quite a relationship, but never quite nothing either. It was undefined, unspoken, yet it pulsed with an intensity that both of them could feel in the silence of their shared glances, the quiet understanding in their moments together.*

*For nearly two years, they had navigated this uncertain space, walking the fine line between what could be and what was. They had grown with each other, their bond evolving in ways that neither of them had anticipated when they first met. It wasn't always easy—there were moments of confusion, of doubt, of wondering where they stood—but through it all, they had remained steadfast, their connection growing stronger with each passing day.*

*For Pandey, Vanya was a constant source of fascination. Every time he saw her, something new was revealed, some hidden depth he had not noticed before. She wasn't just a person to him; she was an entire universe, constantly shifting, constantly unfolding. Her laughter, her wit, her intelligence, even her silences—they all held pieces of a puzzle he longed to solve. Yet, the more he unraveled, the more he realized that she was a puzzle that would never quite be solved. In that realization, he found a strange comfort, a knowledge that he would spend his lifetime learning about her, and that every discovery would only deepen his affection.*

*Vanya, in turn, saw something in Pandey that she couldn't quite place, something that made her feel both grounded and wild at the same time. He was a person who embraced her in all her contradictions, who understood her in ways no one else had. He could make her laugh at the most trivial things, yet challenge her intellectually in a way that made her feel seen and heard. There was a warmth in his presence, a quiet safety that she had never experienced before. He was the calm to her storm, the balance to her restlessness, yet he never tried to change her. He accepted her as she was, and in doing so, he became the anchor that kept her grounded, even when the world around them seemed uncertain.*

*Together, they were a force—neither overwhelming nor passive, but an energy that hummed quietly beneath the surface. It was the way their fingers brushed by accident in crowded hallways, or the way their eyes met across a crowded room, understanding the words left unsaid. It was the way they laughed over silly jokes or shared long conversations about everything and nothing. Each day spent with Vanya was a new adventure for Pandey, one that left him feeling both exhilarated and at peace. She had become his muse, the quiet flame that fueled his desire to understand the complexities of life, love, and everything in between.*

*In Vanya, Pandey saw the light and the shadow, the quiet moments and the bursts of energy, the calm that soothed his soul and the fire that ignited his spirit. She was his constant, his mystery, his muse. And though they had never explicitly labeled what they shared, Pandey didn't need to. He knew, in the quiet spaces between their words, that what they had was something rare, something worth cherishing. It was a love undefined but deeply felt—a love that didn't need to fit into a mold, because it was always something more than that. It was them, together, in a world that was constantly shifting around them, but in each other, they had found a place of stillness. A place where everything made sense, even when nothing else did.*

# CHAPTER SIXTY

# Vanya: The Scholar with a Bright Halo & Pandey: The Campus's All-Rounder

*Vanya was the kind of student who made professors beam with pride and classmates gasp in awe. Her name frequently adorned the dean's list, her answers in class were laced with insight, and she moved through the campus like a comet—dazzling, fleeting, and rare. But there was more to her than her academic brilliance. Beneath her scholarly demeanor lay an ocean of emotions, carefully guarded yet vividly alive. She was a bibliophile, an artist in her private moments, and a dreamer who found poetry in the mundane.*

*Her days were meticulously planned: lectures, library sessions, group discussions, and the occasional break spent sketching in the garden. Yet, there was one element of unpredictability in her otherwise regimented life—Pandey.*

*In stark contrast to Vanya's focused brilliance, Pandey was the quintessential all-rounder. His name wasn't just associated with academics; it echoed through the corridors of the student council office, the sports arena, and even the cultural stage. Charismatic and*

*confident, he had a way of turning heads wherever he went. Yet, beneath the charm and easy laughter was a man of depth, someone who valued connection over conquest and meaning over moments. Pandey excelled at many things, but his real talent lay in people. He had an aura that made others gravitate toward him, whether it was a first-year student seeking guidance or a professor in need of an event organizer. But amid all the chaos of campus life, his anchor was Vanya.*

# CHAPTER SIXTY-ONE

# A Symphony of Silent Understanding

*From the very first day, there was an unspoken understanding between them, something that transcended words. It wasn't love, at least not in the traditional sense, but it was something far more complex, a connection that defied definition. Their eyes would often meet across the lecture hall, and in those fleeting moments, they shared silent hellos, as if their gaze was enough to convey everything they couldn't put into words. It was a dance of glances, a language without sound, yet it said more than any spoken sentence ever could.*

*Between lectures and late-night study sessions, they would walk together to the canteen, the mundane act of getting food transformed into a ritual. Their conversations spanned an eclectic range of topics—from the intricacies of quantum physics to the vibrant buzz surrounding the upcoming campus fest. There was never a sense of rush, no urgency to fill the silences, as their bond existed in the comfortable pauses between words. Yet, in all their discussions, they never once crossed the fragile boundary of verbal confession. They had learned to communicate in ways that went beyond the need for labels or titles. Their connection was akin to a poem—layered, nuanced, and open to interpretation. It didn't need the clarity of a thesis or the certainty of definitions to be profound. It was simply them, woven together in a language all their own.*

*Pandey found himself captivated by Vanya's passion, not just for her studies but for life itself. He loved the way her eyes would light up whenever she delved into a subject that intrigued her. Her enthusiasm was infectious, and he often found himself hanging on her every word, not because he understood the complexities of what she was saying, but because her energy, her brilliance, was magnetic. She wasn't just a student; she was someone who breathed life into every moment, someone who saw beauty in the smallest things. The way she'd lose herself in the details, her fingers absentmindedly tapping on the table as she spoke, was something Pandey treasured. It was in those moments that he saw the depth of who she was—not just the person she appeared to be, but the person she was when no one else was watching.*

*Vanya, in turn, found something equally mesmerizing in Pandey. He was her balance, the unexpected spark in the carefully constructed routine of her life. Where she was methodical, Pandey was spontaneous. Where she sought order, he thrived in chaos. Yet, somehow, they fit together perfectly. She admired the way he could find joy in the simplest things—the warmth of a cup of chai shared in the early morning, the rush of adrenaline during a football match, or the way his eyes would light up as they drove past the campus in the golden hour, the sun casting long shadows over the buildings. For Vanya, those moments were pure magic. The world seemed to slow down when Pandey was around, and in those instances, time didn't matter. It was as if they were two pieces of a puzzle, constantly shifting and evolving, yet always finding a way to fit.*

*Pandey didn't need grand gestures or long speeches. His love for Vanya was in the little things—the quiet way he'd offer her his jacket when she was cold, the gentle teasing he'd throw her way, the shared laughter that echoed through the corridors of their campus. For Vanya, it was in the way he could make the ordinary extraordinary, the way he could find joy in the simplest of things. She saw in him a reminder of everything she'd forgotten to enjoy in the rush of life: the small, fleeting moments that, when seen through his eyes, became something worth savoring.*

*Together, they formed a perfect balance, each completing the other in ways neither of them fully understood. They didn't need to label what they had. It was a relationship of trust and admiration, of shared moments that transcended time and space. It was a connection rooted in quiet understanding, a bond that grew stronger with every laugh, every conversation, every glance shared in the midst of a crowded room. And perhaps, in the end, that was enough.*

# CHAPTER SIXTY-TWO

# The Unwritten Pact

*What made their relationship unique was its silent foundation, an unspoken understanding that ran deeper than any words could express. Neither Pandey nor Vanya ever uttered the words "I love you," nor did they feel the need to. It wasn't that those words were meaningless or unnecessary; it was simply that the depth of their connection transcended verbal affirmation. Their bond was like a river, flowing steadily, carving its path through the landscape of their lives, shaping them in ways neither could fully comprehend. It was a quiet force that neither rushed nor hesitated, a constant undercurrent that guided them even when the world around them seemed chaotic.*

*Their relationship didn't need to be defined by labels or grand gestures. It existed in the small moments, in the shared glances and the gentle touches, in the laughter that echoed through the halls of their college, and in the long conversations that stretched into the early hours of the morning. Every interaction was a testament to their closeness, a deeper connection built not on words, but on understanding. They communicated in ways that went beyond language—through silence, through presence, through the knowledge that they could simply be with each other, no explanations required. It was as if the universe had written their story in invisible ink, visible only to those who knew where to look, a story that was uniquely theirs, unfolding in its own time.*

*The world around them often speculated, unable to grasp the nature of their bond. Friends teased them, asking when they would finally "make it official." Some would joke about them being the perfect couple without ever putting a name to it, while others would glance at them with curiosity, trying to decipher the mystery between them. Yet, Pandey and Vanya never bothered to clarify. They would simply smile, a quiet, knowing smile that spoke volumes. Their eyes would meet, and for a moment, everything else would fade into the background. In that look, there was a world of understanding—an acknowledgment that no one else needed to comprehend their connection because it was perfectly clear to them.*

*For them, their connection didn't need labels or validation. It was enough that they understood each other in ways words could never capture. They didn't need to declare their feelings to the world because, in their hearts, they had already spoken everything that mattered. The weight of their affection was carried in the smallest of gestures—the way Pandey would always ensure Vanya had her favorite snack after a long day, or the way Vanya would quietly listen to Pandey's rambling thoughts, offering him comfort without saying a word.*

*In a world that often demanded certainty, they existed in a space of quiet knowing. Their love wasn't dependent on public acknowledgment or societal expectations. It didn't need to be announced or celebrated in grandiose ways. It was simply enough to be, in the moments they shared, knowing that their bond was real, deep, and infinite. Their relationship was a silent revolution, a quiet defiance of the idea that love must always be spoken to be understood. For Pandey and Vanya, the understanding was in the silence, the absence of need, and the deep connection that flowed effortlessly between them. That was all they ever needed.*

# CHAPTER SIXTY-THREE

# The Twist: A Love Beyond Words

*The twist in their tale came not from conflict or tragedy but from the sheer uniqueness of their bond. In a world obsessed with declarations and grand proposals, they chose to let their actions speak. Pandey's gentle reminders for Vanya to take breaks, Vanya's quiet support during Pandey's moments of self-doubt—these were their love letters to each other.*

*As their college years drew to a close, the question loomed: What next? Would they finally put into words what had remained unspoken for so long? Or would they continue to let their bond evolve in its silent, poetic way? Only time would tell, but one thing was certain—theirs was a love that didn't need to be spoken to be felt. It was a symphony of silent understanding, a twist of tales that defied convention and celebrated the beauty of the unspoken.*

*As time went on, their relationship evolved. It became something unspoken, a bond that neither of them could quite put into words. They were more than just friends, more than just lovers—they were partners in a silent, unacknowledged dance of understanding.*

*Neither Pandey nor Vanya had ever proposed to each other. There were no grand confessions, no pivotal moment where one dropped to their knees and asked the other to spend a lifetime together. Instead, their love grew in the quiet moments—the shared laughter over a cup of coffee, the late-night phone calls that lasted until the early hours of the morning, the knowing glances that spoke volumes.*

*But as time passed, they began to wonder: Were they just caught in a situationship? Was this just a series of coincidences, a beautiful disaster with no clear destination? They never asked each other what they were, never tried to define their relationship with labels. But deep down, they knew they were meant to be together, whether or not they ever put it into words.*

*There were times when Pandey would look at Vanya, his heart swelling with feelings he didn't quite understand. And Vanya, ever the introspective one, would catch his gaze and smile faintly, as though she could see right through him. In those moments, the unspoken words between them were louder than anything they could have said aloud.*

*Yet, despite this deep connection, there was always an undercurrent of uncertainty. They both feared vulnerability, afraid that giving voice to their feelings would make them too real, too fragile. They never asked for labels because they feared that once they labeled it, it would break. So, they let it be—this beautiful, complicated, and messy thing that lived between them.*

# CHAPTER SIXTY-FOUR

# A Magical Journey to Saharanpur : The Decision

*It was a crisp morning in early February, a time when the air carried a subtle promise of spring, with the first hints of warmth melting the winter's chill. The sun, still low on the horizon, cast a soft glow over the college campus, giving the world a quiet, golden hue. Pandey and Vanya sat side by side on a weathered wooden bench near the college canteen, their laughter blending with the lively buzz of student chatter. The sound of footsteps and conversations echoed around them, but in that moment, it felt as though time had slowed just for them.*

*Vanya's eyes sparkled as she animatedly spoke about her plan to visit her home in Saharanpur. She was a natural storyteller, her voice light and easy, flowing like a gentle breeze. She talked about the familiar sights and sounds of her hometown, the bustling markets, the comfort of family dinners, and the feeling of peace that only home could provide.*

*"I'll take the train this weekend," she said, brushing a stray strand of hair behind her ear. "I've missed home, and my attendance is already sorted. I just need to take a few days to recharge."*

*Pandey, ever the attentive listener, leaned back against the bench, his eyes fixed on her as she spoke. He had always loved the way Vanya's eyes lit up when she shared her plans or talked about her dreams. There was something so infectious about her enthusiasm that made him feel like he could conquer the world if only she asked him to. But as she finished her sentence, a thought began to form in his mind, one that would turn their usual routine into something extraordinary. "What if I drop you off instead?" he suggested, his voice tinged with a playful mischief, a grin slowly spreading across his face.*

*Vanya blinked, taken aback by the spontaneity of his suggestion. "You mean by car? That's a long drive, Pandey. Are you sure?" Her tone was skeptical, but there was a spark of curiosity in her eyes, as if the idea was intriguing her.*

*"Absolutely," he replied without hesitation, his voice growing more confident. "Think of it: a long drive, just the two of us. We can stop wherever we like, take detours, explore new places. It'll be an adventure."*

*Vanya couldn't help but laugh, the sound ringing out clear and carefree through the courtyard. "You're crazy," she said between giggles, shaking her head in disbelief. But even as she teased him, the warmth in her smile betrayed her excitement. Pandey had that effect on her—he made the impossible seem effortless, turning even the most mundane moments into something magical.*

*She paused for a moment, her laughter settling into a fond smile as she considered the idea. A road trip with Pandey—no deadlines, no distractions, just the open road ahead of them, and the possibility of sharing new experiences together. It was exactly the kind of adventure she had always wanted, but never thought to ask for.*

*"I guess it could be fun," she said finally, her voice softening. "But we're doing this your way, then. No backing out once we're on the road!"*

*Pandey's grin widened, and he gave a mock salute. "You have my word. It'll be a journey we won't forget."*

*And so, the plan was set. They would drive from the city to Saharanpur together, no rush, no rules. They'd stop for roadside chai, sing along to their favorite songs, and make memories that would last long after the weekend was over. What had started as a simple suggestion now felt like the beginning of something bigger—an opportunity to carve out a space for themselves, away from the world that constantly demanded their attention.*

*As the bell rang, signaling the start of the next class, Vanya stood up, brushing off her skirt and gathering her things. "I'll pack a bag tonight," she said, still smiling. "But you better keep your word, Pandey."*

*"I will," he assured her, standing up to walk alongside her toward the canteen. "Just wait till you see where I take you along the way."*

*As they walked together, the campus around them seemed to fade into the background. For a moment, it was just the two of them, their hearts already on the road ahead, ready for an adventure they hadn't even begun to imagine.*

# CHAPTER SIXTY-FIVE

# The Departure

*Saturday dawned with a pale golden hue, as if the universe itself was blessing the day ahead. The world felt a little quieter in the early morning light, the air crisp with the promise of adventure. Pandey's car, an old but reliable sedan that had seen countless journeys, stood ready in the hostel parking lot. He approached it with an oddly measured precision, checking the tires, filling the tank, and adjusting the mirrors—all the while trying to mask the nervous flutter in his chest. This wasn't just any road trip; this was their road trip, a journey he had been dreaming of for days.*

*Vanya arrived, as if conjured by the morning light, carrying a small bag slung casually over her shoulder. Her face was radiant with anticipation, the kind of smile that lit up the world around her. She tossed a playful glance at Pandey as she approached the car.*

*"Ready, driver?" she teased, her eyes gleaming with excitement as she slid into the passenger seat, buckling up.*

*Pandey, feeling a wave of calm wash over him at her presence, nodded with a grin. "Always," he replied, his voice steady but the rapid beating of his heart betraying his excitement. With a final glance at the rearview mirror, he turned the key in the ignition, and the engine hummed to life, pulling them away from the familiar and into the unknown.*

*The college buildings slowly faded into the distance behind them as they drove out of the city, the hum of the car's engine the only sound between them. The silence wasn't uncomfortable, but rather full of unspoken words and shared smiles. Outside the windows, the scenery shifted, revealing a landscape untouched by the rush of daily life. The road stretched ahead, winding through the countryside, a ribbon of possibility laid before them.*

*Vanya, ever the spontaneous spirit, began to hum a tune, the melody light and carefree. Her voice, though soft, added a layer of warmth to the journey, a perfect companion to the soft breeze that danced through the open window. From time to time, she would point out sights that caught her eye—fields of vibrant yellow mustard flowers, cows grazing lazily in the distance, and quaint villages that seemed suspended in time.*

*"Look at that," Vanya said, her finger tracing the silhouette of a distant mountain. "It's like a painting."*

*Pandey glanced at her, following her gaze, his eyes lingering on the mountains that loomed in the horizon, their peaks veiled in a misty haze. It was beautiful, but more so because she was there beside him, sharing it with him.*

*The fields, painted in shades of green and gold, seemed endless, their gentle curves creating a peaceful rhythm that matched the beat of their hearts. The sky above was the perfect blue of early spring, dotted with wisps of clouds that drifted lazily by. It mirrored their boundless spirits, free from the constraints of schedules and deadlines, moving at their own pace.*

*Pandey found himself looking at Vanya more than he had intended. Her face, lit by the soft glow of the morning sun, was framed by the mess of her hair, which fluttered lightly in the breeze. She was lost in the moment, her eyes scanning the horizon, a contented smile playing at her lips. In that quiet, unspoken way, she was everything he had ever needed and more. He couldn't help but marvel at the thought of having her beside him, not just for this journey, but for the many journeys that lay ahead.*

*For Pandey, the journey wasn't just about reaching Saharanpur or even the adventure they had planned; it was about the fleeting moments spent with Vanya, those small, seemingly insignificant instances that, when strung together, became the essence of love. The way her laughter made him feel as though he could conquer any* challenge. The way her presence filled the car with a warmth that had nothing to do with the weather. The way their conversation flowed effortlessly, sometimes interrupted by comfortable silences that spoke louder than words.

As the miles rolled by, the rhythm of the road became a soundtrack to their growing connection, one that didn't need to be defined or analyzed. It simply existed. It was in the shared glances, the easy banter, the quiet comfort of being together in the vast, open world. Pandey couldn't have imagined a better companion for this journey, for this moment in time. All the days they had spent together had led to this very moment, where the world was theirs to explore, and all that mattered was the space between their hearts.

Pandey stole another glance at Vanya, her face now bathed in the golden light of the sun. She caught his gaze and smiled, a soft, knowing smile that seemed to say everything he had ever wanted to hear. But there was no need for words—this moment, this journey, was all that mattered. And for the first time, Pandey truly understood that the destination wasn't the point. It was the companionship, the shared experiences, and the quiet assurance that whatever lay ahead, they would face it together.

# The Journey

*As the hours passed, the landscape outside the car window shifted from the urban sprawl to the wide-open expanse of the countryside, and with it, the nature of their conversations deepened. What had started as light-hearted banter gradually gave way to more intimate exchanges, the kind of conversations that were reserved for only the most trusted of hearts. Pandey found himself opening up in ways he hadn't expected.*

*He spoke of his dreams—ambitions that stretched far beyond the confines of their college campus, aspirations that once seemed too distant to chase. He spoke of his fears, too, the quiet insecurities that sometimes kept him up at night, the doubts that gnawed at him even in the midst of his confidence. He shared the unspoken vulnerabilities he had kept hidden from the world, the parts of him that only a few, like Vanya, could see.*

*Vanya, ever the attentive listener, was fully present. Her gaze never left him, her eyes filled with a softness that reassured him. Occasionally, she would nod in understanding, offering quiet murmurs of encouragement that allowed him to continue. There was no judgment in her gaze, only a safe space where he could be his truest self. The car's interior, with its soft hum and the occasional swoosh of the wind outside, seemed to cocoon them from the rest of the world. In that moment, Pandey felt as though they were the only two people in existence, sharing not just a ride, but a profound connection that transcended words.*

Then, in a sudden burst of boldness, Vanya leaned over, closing the small gap between them. Her fingers brushed gently against his cheek, sending a shiver down his spine. It was a touch that spoke volumes, tender yet fearless in its affection. Her voice was soft, barely audible over the hum of the engine, but it was more intimate than anything she had said before.

"You're more than I ever thought I deserved, Pandey," she whispered, her words carrying a vulnerability of their own, as though she were offering him a part of her heart that was usually kept locked away.

Pandey's breath caught at her honesty. He turned his head slightly, meeting her gaze, and found that her eyes held a mixture of affection and something deeper—something that hinted at the kind of love that didn't need to be declared aloud to be felt. It was a quiet kind of love, one that existed in every shared moment and every gesture, even the smallest ones. His heart swelled, the kind of fullness that comes from knowing that someone sees you—not just for your strengths, but for your weaknesses, too—and loves you in spite of it all.

Before he could respond, the intimate moment between them was broken by Vanya's mischievous grin. She kissed him softly on the neck, the warmth of her lips lingering for just a moment before pulling away. Her laughter bubbled up from deep within her chest, a light, playful sound that danced in the air around them. It was infectious, and Pandey couldn't help but laugh along, his cheeks flushing as he felt his ears turn bright red.

"Eyes on the road, madam," Pandey quipped, trying—and failing—to maintain focus on the road. His voice held a teasing undertone, though it was clear that his mind was far from the steering wheel. The rush of warmth from her touch, the sweetness of her kiss, and the connection they shared left him momentarily lost in her.

Vanya, not missing a beat, leaned back against the seat, still laughing, though her eyes remained fixed on him. "I think I'll keep you distracted," she said with a wink, her tone daring, yet tender. The playful audacity in her words only deepened the moment, marking it with the youthful energy that was so unique to their relationship.

*Their journey was no longer just about the destination. It was about the boldness of their affection, the willingness to be vulnerable, and the shared sense of freedom that came from being so entirely themselves with each other. The road stretched out before them, winding and ever-changing, much like the path they were walking together in life. With every mile that passed, the intimacy between them grew, and every stolen glance, every touch, every whispered word, only served to reinforce the pull they had on each other.*

*In this moment, the journey felt endless—like an adventure that could go on forever, filled with boldness, laughter, and the intoxicating force of their love.*

# CHAPTER SIXTY-SEVEN

# The Moment

*Hours melted into minutes as Saharanpur loomed closer. Vanya's phone buzzed with a message from her father, confirming that he'd be waiting at the train station. The timing was crucial; they couldn't afford to raise suspicion.*

*Pandey glanced at the clock, calculating the remaining distance. "We're cutting it close," he said, his voice tinged with urgency.*

*"Don't worry," Vanya reassured him, her hand resting on his. "The train's late; we'll make it."*

*The last stretch of the journey was a blur of focused driving and stolen glances. The streets of Saharanpur greeted them with a mix of familiarity and anticipation. As they approached the station, Pandey pulled over a block away. Vanya adjusted her hair and stepped out, her bag slung over her shoulder.*

*"Thank you for everything," she said, leaning in through the open window. Their eyes met, a silent promise passing between them.*

*"Always," Pandey replied, his voice steady despite the ache of parting.*

# The Arrival

*Vanya walked into the station just as her father's eyes lit up at the sight of her. "There you are," he exclaimed. "How was the train?"*

*"Late, as always," Vanya replied with a smile, the lie slipping effortlessly from her lips. She glanced back briefly, knowing Pandey was already on his way back, the road once again his solitary companion.*

*In the car, Pandey replayed the journey in his mind, a bittersweet smile tugging at his lips. The roads that had once seemed unknown were now etched with memories of a magical day spent with Vanya.*

*For both of them, it was a journey full of love, laughter, and fleeting moments of reckless abandon—a day that would remain forever etched in their hearts as a chapter of bold, youthful love.*

# Unpllaned Bonds

*It was mid-year, and life seemed to be flowing smoothly for Vanya Jain. She was thriving at college, enjoying her freedom in the hostel, and spending cherished moments with her love, Pandey. Their relationship was the highlight of her otherwise hectic academic life. The warmth and simplicity of their bond brought a sense of stability amidst the chaos of exams and assignments. But as they say, destiny often has its own plans, and this time, it wasn't playing fair.*

*Unbeknownst to Vanya, her mother was fighting a battle she hadn't shared with her. Diagnosed with breast cancer, her mother had been undergoing treatment quietly. The family had chosen not to inform Vanya, fearing the news would disrupt her focus during the critical exam season. They bore the weight of this secret in silence, shielding her from the storm they were weathering back at home in Indirapuram.*

*One warm evening, Pandey stood outside the hostel gate, sipping on a cold coffee while waiting for Vanya. The familiar sight of her figure approaching brought a smile to his face, but that smile quickly faded when she hugged him tightly and burst into tears. Her sobs were loud, unrestrained, and heartbreaking. Pandey froze, unsure of what had triggered her outburst. He tried to comfort her, rubbing her back gently and murmuring soothing words, but she remained inconsolable.*

*Moments later, one of Vanya's friends arrived, and Pandey finally learned the reason behind her anguish. The news of her mother's illness had just reached her. The family's attempt to shield her had crumbled, and she was now grappling with the heavy burden of reality.*

*Pandey's heart sank as he realized the depth of her pain. He did his best to console her, offering quiet support as she cried in his arms.*

*That evening, Vanya left for her uncle's home in Indirapuram, where her family had gathered. She barely managed a goodbye before getting into the cab, leaving Pandey standing by the curb with an aching heart and a mind full of questions.*

*Days turned into weeks, and Pandey's phone remained silent. He knew better than to intrude. Vanya needed space and time to be with her family. Yet, the distance gnawed at him. He wanted to be there for her, to share her burden, but he understood that this was her family's fight and that his role was to remain a silent pillar of strength from afar.*

*Finally, a message from Vanya arrived. She informed him that her family had decided to continue her mother's treatment in Delhi and that they'd be staying at her uncle's home in Indirapuram for the foreseeable future. She apologized for her absence and explained that she wouldn't be able to attend college for some time. Though her words were brief, Pandey could sense the weight behind them.*

*After the surgery and the initial round of chemotherapy, Pandey decided he couldn't stay away any longer. He wanted to see her, to be there for her in whatever way he could. He bought a bunch of fresh fruits and coconut water, essentials he thought might help in her mother's recovery, and made his way to the hospital.*

*Pandey detested hospitals. The sterile smell, the somber faces, and the oppressive air of suffering made him uneasy. He would avoid them at all costs, even when unwell. Yet, this time, his resolve was stronger than his discomfort. For Vanya, he could endure anything.*

*Walking into the hospital, Pandey's heart pounded as he approached the room where Vanya's family was gathered. This was his first time meeting her parents and elder brother, a meeting that neither he nor they had planned or expected.*

*Inside the room, Vanya's mother lay on the hospital bed, her face pale but her spirit unmistakably strong. Her father sat beside her, holding her hand, while Vanya's elder brother, whom she fondly called "Bhaiyu," stood by the window, staring out in quiet contemplation.*

*When Vanya saw Pandey at the door, her face lit up with a mixture of surprise and relief. "Pandey!" she exclaimed softly, rushing to him. The tension in the room eased slightly as he stepped in, his presence bringing a flicker of warmth.*

*"Namaste," Pandey greeted her parents respectfully, placing the fruits and coconut water on a nearby table.*

*Vanya's father nodded, his expression a blend of gratitude and curiosity. "You must be Pandey," he said, his voice measured.*

*Pandey nodded. "Yes, sir. I'm a friend of Vanya's. I heard about the situation and wanted to... to offer any help I can." His words felt inadequate, but they were sincere.*

*Her mother smiled weakly. "Thank you for coming, beta. It means a lot."*

*Pandey's gaze softened as he looked at her. "How are you feeling, aunty?" he asked gently.*

*"Better now," she replied, her voice faint but steady. "The doctors are hopeful. We're taking it one day at a time."*

*Pandey nodded, his respect for her resilience growing. He turned to Bhaiyu, who had been observing him silently. "It's nice to meet you," Pandey said, extending his hand.*

*Bhaiyu shook it firmly, a hint of a smile breaking through his otherwise serious demeanor. "Same here," he said simply.*

*The awkwardness of the situation lingered, but Pandey's genuine demeanor slowly dissolved it. He sat with the family for a while, listening as they talked about the treatment, the doctors, and their hopes for recovery. He didn't try to dominate the conversation or offer unwarranted advice; he simply listened and supported.*

*Before leaving, Pandey revealed a special gift he had brought for Vanya's mother. He handed her a carefully wrapped package, which contained a portrait of her that he had drawn himself. Along with the portrait was a handwritten note that read:*

**"Taqdeer si dikhti hai, Jamane mein rehti hai, khawabon sa gharounda jiska, Bachpan si Khilti hai."**
**(By: Hritik yogesh Pandey)**

*Vanya's mother's eyes glistened with tears as she held the portrait and read the note. "You're an artist and a poet too?" she asked, her voice tinged with admiration.*

*Pandey smiled shyly. "I dabble a little, aunty. I thought this might bring a smile to your face."*

*"It does," she said, her voice breaking slightly. "It's beautiful. Thank you."*

*Later, when Vanya walked him out, she looked at him with tears in her eyes. "Thank you for coming," she whispered.*

*Pandey smiled softly. "You don't have to thank me. I'm here for you, always."*

*As he left the hospital, Pandey couldn't shake the weight of the meeting. It wasn't how he'd envisioned meeting Vanya's family for the first time, but it had given him a deeper understanding of her world, her struggles, and her strength.*

# CHAPTER SEVENTY

# When Hearts Collide in Quiet Strength

*Beneath the hospital's sterile glow,*
*A tale of resilience began to grow.*
*A mother lay with courage bright,*
*Her spirit a beacon in the night.*
*Her daughter, burdened by hidden pain,*
*Faced the storm, her tears like rain.*
*Yet by her side stood a steady hand,*
*A love unspoken, quiet, and grand.*
*Pandey arrived, with trembling resolve,*
*Through chaos and care, his fears dissolved.*
*A portrait he brought, drawn with care,*
*A token of hope to ease despair.*
*Lines of poetry graced the fragile frame,*
*Whispering strength, softly by name.*
*In "Taqdeer si dikhti hai," he penned,*
*a message of faith to gently mend.*
*In moments unplanned, bonds were made,*
*Through trials endured and prayers conveyed.*
*Destiny's hand may shift and bend,*
*But love and hope will always transcend.*
*Through tears and strength, they stood as one,*
*Until the morning replaced the sun.*
*For though life bends, it does not break,*

*When hearts collide for others' sake.*
*" Life had thrown them into a situation neither of them had*
*anticipated, but together, they would face it—one day at a time. "*

• 203 •

# CHAPTER SEVENTY-ONE

# The Unfolding Drama

*But even stars, so bright and bold,*
*Carry shadows that creep and fold.*
*Pandey's mind, a battlefield wide,*
*Fought wars within he couldn't confide.*
*Questions loomed, unspoken fears,*
*Worries whispered in midnight tears.*
*Was her fire too wild for him to hold?*
*Was their story fleeting—a tale untold?*
*In the silence of his room, when all was still,*
*Pandey wrestled with doubts, heart aching, yet ill.*
*Could he ever be enough for her light?*
*Could he keep her close, without dimming her might?*
*Her passion, a tempest, a force so untamed,*
*Could he be the anchor, or was he too maimed?*
*He feared the distance, the spaces between,*
*The moments where silence might turn into mean.*
*What if, in time, she saw through the veil,*
*And realized their love was destined to fail?*
*Would her fire burn too hot to sustain?*
*Would he, forever, remain just the same?*
*The weight of her laughter, so sweet in the day,*
*Could it become burdensome—leading her astray?*
*He loved her more than words could ever say,*
*But could he hold her, when shadows would play?*
*Would the edges of their bond begin to fray,*

*Or would love conquer the doubts that led him astray?*
*In the quiet of the night, he'd ask himself why,*
*Why do the brightest hearts sometimes fear the sky?*
*Was it the knowledge that all things must bend,*
*That no star can shine without its end?*
*But still, he hoped—despite all his fears,*
*That love could withstand what time might tear.*
*Pandey knew, deep in his soul,*
*That even broken hearts could become whole.*
*Though shadows lingered, as all shadows do,*
*The fire within him, for her, burned true.*
*And maybe, just maybe, that was enough,*
*For their love to endure, tender and tough.*

# CHAPTER SEVENTY-TWO

# Falling Apart

*Then came the days of growing divide,*
*Love's fire dimmed, though they both tried.*
*Words were scarce, yet tempers flew,*
*Old comforts felt foreign, new struggles grew.*
*And in a moment—an unkind twist,*
*A love so deep fell into mist.*
*Vanya, bold, was the first to leave,*
*Pandey remained, alone to grieve.*
*The silence that followed was heavy, profound,*
*A void in his heart that no voice could resound.*
*He wandered through days, a ghost of his past,*
*Each memory a shadow, so bitter, so vast.*
*Their laughter, once bright, now seemed so far,*
*As if the light had dimmed from the very stars.*
*Vanya, who once held his world with a glance,*
*Now drifted away, like a distant dance.*
*He wondered where her heart had gone,*
*And if she felt the same ache, the same dawn.*
*But pride had built walls, too high to climb,*
*And time, relentless, was stealing their prime.*
*She, too, fought her demons, the pain she concealed,*
*Her heart caught between love and what it had healed.*
*She missed him in moments, in silence so deep,*
*But knew that the distance was hers to keep.*
*A love that once flourished, now fragile and torn,*

*Left both of them haunted, alone and forlorn.*
*The days felt longer, the nights even worse,*
*Pandey's thoughts turned to verses, to poetry's curse.*
*He poured his sorrow into ink-stained lines,*
*Writing of love lost, of fractured signs.*
*But no rhyme could heal the wound in his chest,*
*No metaphor could make the ache feel less.*
*Vanya, too, sought solace in fleeting things,*
*Trying to forget what her heart still clings.*
*The freedom she sought was both sweet and bitter,*
*Yet deep down, she yearned for the love that glittered.*
*But fear of the unknown held her in place,*
*Afraid of losing more than what they'd embraced.*
*And so they drifted, like leaves in the breeze,*
*Both longing, both grieving, both searching for ease.*
*A love once whole, now scattered and torn,*
*Yet somehow still pulsing, though both were forlorn.*

# CHAPTER SEVENTY-THREE

# The Haunting Shadows

*Now, years have passed, yet Pandey remains,*
*A prisoner of love's sweet, bitter chains.*
*He's trapped in memories, their fragrant hue,*
*Her voice, her touch, the laughter he knew.*
*He writes of her, but his pen shakes,*
*Sings of love, but his voice breaks.*
*Each word a battle, each song a tear,*
*Haunted by a love he held so dear.*
*The years have carved lines into his face,*
*But her absence, still, he cannot erase.*
*He walks through life like a shadow on air,*
*Searching for her in places unaware.*
*The touch of another, the laugh of a friend,*
*Can never fill the void, can never mend.*
*He often finds himself lost in the night,*
*In the silence where once her laughter took flight.*
*Her name is a whisper, a ghost on his tongue,*
*A melody unsung, a song left undone.*
*No matter how far he tries to move on,*
*Her image, her essence, lingers like dawn.*
*He catches glimpses of her in the crowd,*
*In a stranger's smile, in a voice too loud.*
*But it's never her, never the same,*
*Yet he clings to it all, playing the game.*
*He's haunted, yet yearns for the haunting to cease,*

*To find peace, to find his release.*
*The love they shared was a fierce, wild thing,*
*And now it haunts him like an eternal spring.*
*His heart is a garden, overrun with regret,*
*A place where their love will never forget.*
*He plucks the petals of memories worn,*
*But each one reminds him of love torn.*
*He writes letters, he'll never send,*
*Hoping one day, the sorrow will end.*
*But no matter how many words he writes,*
*He can never bring back those summer nights.*
*She was his muse, his light, his fire,*
*Now she is the smoke that fuels his desire.*
*In the quiet hours, when no one's around,*
*He feels her presence, an ethereal sound.*
*And though he's moved forward, tried to break free,*
*Her absence remains, a part of his plea.*
*The love they once shared—too beautiful to be—*
*Now forever lives in the silence he'll never set free.*

# The Reflection

*Pandey, the boy who once adored,*
*Now lives in moments they once explored.*
*Time has moved, yet he stands still,*
*A heart divided, against its will.*
*Vanya, fierce, now a memory blurred,*
*Her wild essence, his heart's preferred.*
*Though apart, she lingers near,*
*A shadow of love he holds so clear.*
*The world around him spins and bends,*
*But in his mind, the past never ends.*
*Her laughter still echoes in his ears,*
*A melody sweet, now mixed with tears.*
*The days they spent, the nights they shared,*
*In every corner, he still finds her there.*
*Her gaze, her touch, a ghost of the past,*
*A love too deep to ever outlast.*
*He wanders through life, a restless soul,*
*Chasing fragments that never make him whole.*
*A smile from a stranger, a laugh that rings,*
*For a moment, he feels the stir of old things.*
*But it's never quite the same, never the spark,*
*Her absence has left him lost in the dark.*
*Vanya, fierce and free, was the flame,*
*The fire in his heart that called her name.*
*But now, all he's left with are the embers,*

*Fading memories that time remembers.*
*Her wild spirit, her untamed grace,*
*Lingers like a shadow he can't erase.*
*He tries to move on, to love again,*
*But no one can hold his heart like when*
*Her fingers traced the paths of his soul,*
*Filling the cracks, making him whole.*
*Now, he clings to the shadows of her smile,*
*Living in the past, going the extra mile.*
*She was his chaos, his calm, his muse,*
*The one he couldn't lose.*
*Now, her absence is a wound that won't heal,*
*A constant ache he cannot conceal.*
*And though he's learned to live without her touch,*
*Pandey's heart still longs for her too much.*
*She's not gone; she's never far,*
*A love so deep, it remains a scar.*
*A shadow that stretches through his days,*
*Her presence forever weaving its ways.*
*In every thought, in every dream,*
*Vanya lives on, like a fading beam.*
*Pandey, the boy who once adored,*
*Now lives in moments they once explored.*
*And though time has moved and hearts have grown,*
*His love for her remains, etched in stone.*
*For in his heart, Vanya will always stay,*
*A part of him, forever and a day.*

# CHAPTER SEVENTY-FIVE

# The Redemption's Wishper

*Perhaps one day, Pandey will find,*
*A love that heals his fractured mind.*
*A soul to mend the broken seams,*
*A heart to rekindle fading dreams.*
*But until that day, his heart stays chained,*
*A prisoner of love's joy and pain.*
*For though he seeks a new embrace,*
*It's Vanya's memory he cannot erase.*
*His pen and paper remain his guide,*
*A silent witness to the love he can't hide.*
*With ink-stained fingers, he writes and weeps,*
*Pouring his soul into verses so deep.*
*Each line a cry, each word a sigh,*
*A tribute to the girl who made him fly.*
*Her spirit lingers, soft and near,*
*In the rhythm of his thoughts, so clear.*
*Through endless nights, he writes his fears,*
*And scribbles poems through falling tears.*
*In every verse, she's still his muse,*
*A love he lost but could never lose.*
*He captures moments that never were,*
*Paints them in colors of love's pure stir.*
*A kiss that never came, a touch that's missed,*

*In his writing, Vanya still exists.*
*The words he writes are filled with ache,*
*But in the pain, a love does wake.*
*A love that never truly died,*
*Though it's buried deep, it still resides.*
*Pandey's heart, though cracked and torn,*
*Finds solace in the poetry born.*
*For even in loss, there is grace,*
*In every verse, her name's embraced.*
*Yet, the world moves on, as worlds do,*
*And Pandey wonders if she'll find someone new.*
*He hopes she's happy, he hopes she's whole,*
*Even if she's no longer the keeper of his soul.*
*For love, like time, doesn't stand still,*
*And hearts, no matter what, must heal.*
*But Pandey's love for her remains,*
*A quiet storm that still sustains.*
*Their story—a bittersweet refrain,*
*A song of joy, of loss, of pain.*
*A melody that never fades,*
*A tale of love, in ink and shades.*
*For in every tear that falls like rain,*
*Vanya's love will still remain.*
*Their love, though distant, still survives,*
*A testament to the way love thrives.*
*Perhaps one day, Pandey will find,*
*A love that heals his fractured mind.*
*But until that day, he'll keep her close,*
*In the quiet corners where memory flows.*
*His heart may mend, but it will always ache,*
*For the love of a lifetime he cannot forsake.*
*And in every poem, in every rhyme,*
*Pandey will carry Vanya through time.*

# CHAPTER SEVENTY-SIX

# The Bond Deepens

*Their connection grew, not carved in stone,*
*But woven in whispers, in moments alone.*
*Her sharp edges met his soothing balm,*
*Their chemistry vibrant, their souls calm.*
*The world around them buzzed with questions,*
*Curiosity growing, fueled by their confessions.*
*"Are they together?" the rumors abound,*
*Yet no words were spoken, no answers found.*
*For their love wasn't bound by labels or time,*
*It was a melody played in rhythm, sublime.*
*A bond so pure, it defied what could be said,*
*More a feeling than a path they'd tread.*
*In the silence between them, truth bloomed,*
*In the absence of definitions, their hearts consumed.*
*A connection stronger than any name,*
*An unspoken promise, a steady flame.*
*On a jail visit, her tears found his hand,*
*A moment of vulnerability, quiet yet grand.*
*Her distress, a storm she couldn't quell,*
*Her heart heavy, her world a shell.*
*But in Pandey, she found a refuge true,*
*A rock in the chaos, a sky so blue.*
*He held her hand with gentle grace,*
*His eyes soft, his heart a steady place.*

*With Avi beside them, they sat that night,*
*In the warmth of their presence, in the chill of fright.*
*The cold could not touch them, nor the doubt,*
*For in their shared silence, love came out.*
*Pandey spoke little, but his touch said more,*
*His presence a balm, her spirit restored.*
*Vanya, with eyes red from tears,*
*Found solace in him, vanishing her fears.*
*In that moment, the world outside fell away,*
*And what mattered was the here, the now, the stay.*
*Their love, unspoken, wrapped them tight,*
*Shielding them from the storm that night.*
*The world could question, could wonder and guess,*
*But in their hearts, they held no need to impress.*
*For the bond they shared was built on trust,*
*A love undefined, but pure and just.*
*As the night deepened, the stars witnessed their silence,*
*A testament to a love born of resilience.*
*The warmth between them was enough to heal,*
*To quiet the world and help them feel.*
*The jail, the distance, the pain and the strain,*
*All faded away, in love's steady refrain.*

# Situationship Defined

*He use to call Vanya, her **"Bivi,"** a jest, a truth,*
*For labels failed their tender youth.*
*A word, a whisper, simple yet profound,*
*A name that held their worlds unbound.*
*In every syllable, an inside joke,*
*A bond that laughter and love provoked.*
*No need for definitions, no need for claim,*
*They were beyond the world's narrow frame.*
*A relationship forged in circumstance's flow,*
*Of jealous sparks and love's afterglow.*
*The fire of youth, both wild and bold,*
*A story of passion, in silver and gold.*
*In moments of tension, in whispered desire,*
*Their connection burned like an eternal fire.*
*They didn't need the world to understand,*
*For what they had was written by hand.*
*Her moods were storms he learned to brave,*
*Her laughter, the treasure his heart would crave.*
*When the clouds rolled in and her heart turned cold,*
*He stood steadfast, unshaken, his grip firm and bold.*
*Through every tempest, he remained the calm,*
*A steady presence, a soothing balm.*
*Her storms, though fierce, couldn't break their bond,*
*For in her eyes, he found a world beyond.*

*He, the anchor to her drifting tide,*
*She, the fire he sheltered inside.*
*Her spirit, untamed, a raging sea,*
*Wild, unpredictable, a force to be.*
*Yet in his arms, she found her rest,*
*A place where her chaos could be its best.*
*He gave her freedom, he gave her space,*
*But in his love, she found her place.*
*She was the flame that lit his soul,*
*The warmth that made him feel whole.*
*Her fire, untamable, fierce and bright,*
*But he was the keeper of her light.*
*Where she burned, he cooled the flame,*
*Where she soared, he gave her aim.*
*They were different, yet intertwined,*
*Two souls that fate had aligned.*
*In their quiet moments, away from the world,*
*They spoke without words, their love unfurled.*
*She didn't need to say it; he could see,*
*The way her heart whispered, "You're home to me."*
*And in the depths of his own gaze,*
*She found a love that could never fade.*
*Their bond, a quiet symphony,*
*Of fire and tide, of you and me.*
*They didn't need the world to explain,*
*What they shared was worth the pain.*
*For in each other, they found a truth,*
*A love beyond the bounds of youth.*
*A connection born of earth and sky,*
*A love that would never say goodbye.*

# A Twist of Fate & A Pinch by Fate

*Fate, the trickster, played its hand,*
*She returned, now wearing another band.*
*The ring on her finger gleamed, a symbol of change,*
*Yet her presence in his life felt haunting, strange.*
*Once, she had been his world, his only desire,*
*Now, she was a memory, a fading fire.*
*Her eyes, once filled with love, now held a quiet sorrow,*
*As though she too mourned what they couldn't borrow.*
*Married, yet her presence near,*
*A haunting melody to his silent tear.*
*Her laughter, once the music of his days,*
*Now echoed in his heart in sorrowful ways.*
*He'd see her across the room, smiling, content,*
*And for a fleeting moment, his world would be rent.*
*The love they had, now buried beneath,*
*A ghost that lingered, quiet, beneath.*
*It wasn't anger, nor regret he felt,*
*But a profound ache, like a wound never healed.*
*On roads, in markets, their paths would meet,*
*A fleeting glance, his heart's defeat.*
*In the crowded streets, amidst the noise,*
*Their eyes would lock, silencing all joys.*
*A brief exchange, a nod, a smile,*

*But the distance between them stretched a mile.*
*Her wedding band, a painful reminder,*
*Of a love lost to time, a past growing kinder.*
*She was there, yet not really present,*
*A piece of his heart forever absent.*
*For her shadow lingered, a quiet pain,*
*A love that lived, though it couldn't remain.*
*Her essence, though veiled in another's arms,*
*Still carried the echoes of their shared charms.*
*Every corner of the town whispered her name,*
*Each familiar place, a reminder of the flame.*
*He'd drive by their old café, the place they used to go,*
*And the memories would come flooding, slow.*
*The taste of her lips, the warmth of her skin,*
*The tenderness of the love they'd once been in.*
*And yet, despite the years, despite the change,*
*He couldn't let go, though his heart was strange.*
*For she was a part of him, woven so tight,*
*That even in her absence, she felt so right.*
*It wasn't just love that had slipped through his grasp,*
*But a connection, eternal, forever to last.*
*He tried to move on, to forget the past,*
*But her shadow was one that would always last.*
*In the silence of the night, he'd often recall,*
*The warmth of her touch, the rise and the fall.*
*How they had once dreamed, hand in hand,*
*Now those dreams were buried in the shifting sand.*
*Yet, as he saw her, with her new life to keep,*
*He knew a part of her was still his to reap.*
*For no matter how far, no matter how deep,*
*A love once rooted would forever creep.*
*Their love, though gone, was never truly erased,*
*It lived in the moments they couldn't replace.*
*It danced in the spaces between the words they never said,*
*A love immortal, still alive in his head.*

*She wore another band, and yet she wore his heart too,*
*A paradox that time never quite knew.*
*They could never go back, nor could they move on,*
*But their story, a song, would forever live on.*

# CHAPTER SEVENTY-NINE

# Unfinished Symphony

*Their story remains, a stanza untold,*
*A tapestry frayed, its threads of gold.*
*Love unfulfilled, yet deeply felt,*
*A bond unbroken, though time has knelt.*
*Hritik walks with her echo in his chest,*
*A love that chaos could not wrest.*
*For sometimes, love is not to last,*
*But to teach, to burn, to craft the past.*

# CHAPTER EIGHTY

# A Conflicted Mind

*Pandey tries to write. The act, once so natural, now feels foreign, like trying to speak in a language he's forgotten. His thoughts are a cacophony—half-formed ideas colliding with memories of betrayal. "Why does this feel so distant, so detached?" he mutters to himself, the echo of his voice filling the void. The words he manages to write feel alien, as though they belong to someone else.*

*He reads them back and feels no connection, no resonance. It's as if his pen has been hijacked by an imposter, and he's left wondering whether his words ever truly belonged to him. The once-familiar act of writing now feels like an act of estrangement, deepening his sense of loss.*

# CHAPTER EIGHTY-ONE

# The Dance of Doubt

*Doubt has become his constant companion, creeping into every corner of his thoughts.*

*Was his talent ever real, or was it merely a reflection of her presence in his life? Had his words always been hers, shaped by her influence and approval?*

*The questions swirl, unanswered, feeding the growing chasm between him and his art.*

*Pandey tries to channel his confusion into poetry, hoping to find clarity through the act of creation. But the verses that emerge feel hollow, their rhythm offbeat, their meaning elusive.*

*He crumples the paper and tosses it aside, frustration bubbling beneath his calm exterior. "Is this who I've become? A writer who can't write, a poet who's lost his rhyme?"*

# CHAPTER EIGHTY-TWO

# The Burden Of Betrayal

*Her betrayal looms large in his mind, a shadow that colors everything he attempts to create. He cannot write about love without recalling the pain of her departure. He cannot pen words of hope without feeling the sting of his own disillusionment.*

*Even his attempts to write about loss feel inadequate, as though the depth of his sorrow is beyond the reach of language.*

*Pandey's pen falters under the weight of his emotions. The words that once came so easily now feel forced,*

*their authenticity lost. He wonders if his art has become a reflection of his fractured soul—a mirror that shows only cracks and distortions. The betrayal has not just taken her away from him; it has taken away his ability to express himself, leaving him voiceless in the face of his own pain.*

# CHAPTER EIGHTY-THREE

# Reflection of The Inner Turmoil

*In the confines of his fractured mind,*
*Pandey fought battles, undefined.*
*A ceaseless war, both loud and mute,*
*A song of pain, a broken lute.*
*The whispers came in shadows' guise,*
*With questions sharp, and endless whys.*
*"Why wasn't I enough? What did I miss?"*
*Each doubt a dagger, each thought amiss.*
*His nights were long, haunted by the past,*
*Memories that never seemed to last.*
*He saw her face, her eyes full of fire,*
*Yet now, all he had was a burning desire.*
*To understand, to know, to feel her touch,*
*But all he had were questions, too much.*
*His heart ached for answers, for closure,*
*But every door seemed a mirage, a phantom exposure.*
*He'd pace the room, his steps unsure,*
*Seeking solace, but finding no cure.*
*Every shadow seemed to whisper her name,*
*Like a melody that stirred up the same flame.*
*How could love fade so quickly, so fast?*
*Was it ever real, or was it just a mask?*
*The world seemed to mock him, so cruel, so cold,*

Leaving him to wonder if their love was ever bold.
A labyrinth of blame, regret, and fear,
Each corner hiding Vanya's sneer.
He couldn't escape the image of her eyes,
That once held love, now filled with lies.
Had he failed her? Was he too late?
Was he never enough to meet her fate?
He longed for the answers that never came,
But all he found was an eternal flame.
He stood by the window, staring at the night,
As the wind whispered secrets in the pale moonlight.
Every gust, every breeze, reminded him of her,
Of moments that once were, now lost to the blur.
Her absence, like a chasm, deep and wide,
A void in his heart he could never hide.
He wanted to scream, to tear at the sky,
But all he could do was silently cry.
He thought of their laughs, their stolen glances,
Of the way her smile gave him second chances.
But now, all he had was silence and space,
And the fading memory of her warm embrace.
What had they been? What had they lost?
Why did love always come at such a cost?
And yet, amid the chaos of his mind,
Pandey searched for peace he couldn't find.
The questions lingered, the pain remained,
But in his heart, a fragile hope was sustained.
He didn't know if he'd ever heal,
If the wounds would close, or if they'd feel real.
But deep inside, a part of him believed,
That someday, somehow, he might be freed.
Until then, he'd live in the quiet storm,
Where love and loss both were reborn.
A fractured mind, a heart that bled,
A soul that wondered if it could ever be led.

*Pandey fought on, in darkness and light,*
*Hoping that one day, he'd find the might*
*To heal his heart, to let go of the past,*
*And find peace in a love that could finally last.*

# The Drama Within

*There were nights he screamed, unheard, unseen,*
*In the theater of his mind, she played the queen.*
*Scenes of betrayal, scripted anew,*
*Each one cutting, each one untrue.*
*Her laughter mocked, her smile betrayed,*
*A haunting echo that never swayed.*
*He'd argue with himself, his logic torn,*
*Between love's beauty and trust's forlorn.*
*Pandey, the hero, Pandey, the fool,*
*Both played parts in memory's cruel school.*
*His pen, once a weapon, now lay still,*
*A soldier lost to his own will.*
*Anger would rise, a fiery storm,*
*A demand for justice, a plea to transform.*
*"Why did she lie? How could she leave?"*
*The rage burned hot, but could not relieve.*
*Then came the love, soft and sweet,*
*A memory of her, their hearts in sync beat.*
*He'd hate her, then love her, then hate again,*
*A vicious cycle, a looping refrain.*

# CHAPTER EIGHTY-FIVE

# The Mirror's Mockery &
# The Ceaseless War

*The mirror became his silent foe,*
*Reflecting a man he didn't know.*
*Dark circles framed eyes that once shone,*
*A shadow of the boy who faced the unknown.*
*"What's wrong with me?" he'd softly say,*
*"Why can't I let her drift away?"*
*The drama played on, a one-man show,*
*An endless tide, an ebb and flow.*
*In the quiet hours, his pen would quake,*
*As he tried to write, his heart would ache.*
*Words came as fragments, thoughts unclear,*
*A language of loss, written in fear.*
*He fought to reclaim his voice, his art,*
*To stitch together his broken heart.*
*But each attempt felt hollow, untrue,*
*A betrayal of the Pandey he once knew.*
*The issues lived, a constant hum,*
*Like an unsung song, or a beating drum.*
*A mind at war, a heart in chains,*
*Pandey bore the scars of love's remains.*

*He knew not peace, he knew not rest,*
*Each battle within, a trial, a test.*
*Yet still, he stood, though broken, worn,*
*A fighter lost, yet not fully torn.*

# CHAPTER EIGHTY-SIX

# A Glimmer of Recognition

*In moments of clarity, when the fog of pain momentarily lifts, Pandey comes to a realization that feels both terrifying and liberating: his struggle is not only about the loss of Vanya, but about his own identity, his own essence as an artist. The absence of her presence—the muse he had once relied upon—has forced him to confront the deep-rooted uncertainties he'd long avoided.*

*For so long, he had believed that his creativity was intertwined with her—the way her laughter would spark his thoughts, how her mere presence would make the words flow with ease. He had painted his world in shades of her: her eyes, her smile, the way she spoke, the way she looked at him. His art had been a mirror to their shared moments, each line, each word, a reflection of the life they had built together. But now, that world was gone. She had slipped away, leaving behind a silence he didn't know how to fill.*

*Pandey's thoughts become tangled in the question that now hangs over him like a stormcloud: Was his art dependent on her, on the external validation that her love had provided? Was it only her presence, her support, that had breathed life into his words? Or was there something deeper within him—some wellspring of creativity that was independent of anyone or anything? Could he find inspiration again, not from the outside world, but from the depths of his own soul?*

*These questions linger like echoes, offering no immediate answers, no easy comfort. But within the uncertainty, there is a spark—a glimmer of hope that flickers, however faint. In the midst of his grief and confusion, Pandey begins to realize that perhaps the loss of Vanya, painful as it is, is an opportunity to rediscover himself. Perhaps this is the moment when he must break free from the external source of his creativity and learn to trust the well of inspiration that resides deep within him.*

*The pen, which once felt foreign in his hand, begins to take on a new weight. It is no longer just an instrument to capture the love and moments he once shared with Vanya, but a tool to unlock a new chapter of his own story. He wonders if he can once again allow the pen to become an extension of his soul, not as a reflection of what was lost, but as a testament to what he has yet to discover.*

*There is no roadmap, no clear path forward, but for the first time in a long while, Pandey feels the faint stirrings of something powerful—an urge to write, to create, not because he has to, but because he simply can.*

*As the days pass, he finds himself sitting by the window once more, the same pen in his hand, but this time with a sense of cautious optimism. The blank page before him is no longer a void, but a possibility. Perhaps, just perhaps, he can learn to build something new, something that belongs entirely to him. A story that is his alone to tell, untethered from the shadows of the past.*

*In this quiet moment of introspection, Pandey realizes that even in the absence of his muse, there is still art to be made. And that, in itself, is a form of reclaiming his own heart, his own identity, and his own future.*

# CHAPTER EIGHTY-SEVEN

# The Path Forward

*Pandey knows that the journey will not be easy.*
*He must learn to write not as a reflection of someone else but as an expression of his own truth.*
*He must confront the pain and betrayal that have silenced his pen and transform them into sources of strength.*
*His words must become his own again, not borrowed or stolen from the memories of another.*
*He picks up his pen, hesitates, and then begins to write. The words are shaky at first, hesitant and uncertain. But as the ink flows, so does a small measure of clarity.*
*He writes not for an audience, not for a muse, but for himself — for the Pandey who once found solace and joy in the act of creation. It is a tentative step, but it is a step nonetheless.*

**-- Pandey's writings may never feel the same, and he may never fully understand the mystery of her betrayal. But he knows that his identity as a writer is not dependent on anyone else. His pen, though estranged, is still his. And as he writes, he begins to rediscover the voice that was always there, waiting for him to claim it once more. ""**

**When my writings rise, a storm they bring,**
**A tempest of thoughts, a heart-wrought sting.**
**"Pandey," they whisper with voices untamed,**
**"Satisfy your soul, leave society unnamed."**
**I pause, I listen, but the echo remains,**
**A chorus of questions, each leaving its stains.**

*They beckon to dreams yet to be fulfilled,*
*A canvas of chaos, where silence is stilled.*
*The writings command, their tone so firm,*
*"Forget the faces, the voices, the term.*
*This person you imagine, this fleeting trace,*
*They'll vanish like shadows in memory's embrace."*
*Yet, the overthinking, relentless and vast,*
*Spins tales of the future, drags chains from the past.*
*Each thought a prisoner, a whispering plea,*
*Caught in the net of what could and will be.*
*I, the thinker, the dreamer undone,*
*Become the neglected, the solitary one.*
*Neither thought nor writing heeds my plight,*
*They're locked in a battle, their ceaseless fight.*
*"Why won't you listen?" I cry to the void,*
*But my voice is drowned, my hope destroyed.*
*The writings, they churn with fervor and zeal,*
*Ignoring the ache of what I feel.*
*One thought suggests, "Give love its chance."*
*Another commands, "Break free, take a stance!"*
*My heart a courtroom, each side debates,*
*While my spirit drifts through uncertain fates.*
*And there I stand, a soul in between,*
*Torn by the battles of the seen and unseen.*
*"Write for yourself," my pen implores,*
*Yet the world's judgment beats down my doors.*
*The writings scold, "Pandey, let it go!*
*Seek no approval, let creativity flow."*

*But thoughts retort with a bitter hiss,*
*"What of rejection?*
*What of dismiss?"*
*In this symphony of mind, no tune is clear,*
*Each note a burden, a shadow of fear.*

*Yet within the chaos, a truth does gleam,*
*That perhaps this struggle is part of the dream.*
*For the neglected one, though silenced, grows,*
*From the fertile soil where conflict sows.*
*Each ignored plea, each unheard cry,*
*Builds a strength unseen beneath the sky.*
*The writings and thoughts may clash and fight,*
*But within the darkness, I find a light.*
*A whisper of peace amidst the fray,*
*A glimmer of dawn at the edge of day.*
*"Pandey," they say, "you are not lost,*
*Each tear you shed has paid the cost.*
*For the soul's freedom is a price well earned,*
*Through fires of doubt, where hearts are burned."*
*So I pick up the pen, though hands do shake,*
*And write for the soul, not for society's sake.*
*Let the thoughts rage on, let them confound,*
*For in this war, my truth is found.*
*No longer neglected, I claim my space,*
*Amidst the turmoil, I find my grace.*

*A dance with chaos, a truce with pain,*
*And in my writings, I live again.*
*I learn that the conflict was never my foe,*
*But a mirror reflecting where I must go.*
*The overthinking, a tangled maze,*
*Leads to truth in its convoluted ways.*
*The soul, neglected, begins to bloom,*
*Casting light through the inner gloom.*
*A garden grows where ashes lay,*
*Colors emerge in shades of gray.*
*I find redemption in every tear,*
*In every doubt, in every fear.*
*For they shaped the path, carved the way,*
*To the peace I cherish today.*

*No longer do I write for their eyes,*
*For society's gaze, or its fleeting highs.*
*I write for the soul, its boundless call,*
*A universe within, a world where I'm all.*
*The neglected one is no more forlorn,*
*For from inner battles, new strength is born.*

*Each conflict faced, a wisdom earned,*
*Each scar a story, each bridge unburned.*
*The writings still rise, but now they sing,*
*Of redemption's grace and the hope it brings.*

*"Pandey," they echo, "you've found your voice,*
*A symphony of freedom, a soul's true choice."*
*The neglected one, no longer torn,*
*Stands whole and radiant, reborn.*
*Through overthinking, I found my art,*
*A pen, a soul, a mended heart.*
*""*

*There was a time when my writings were my solace—a sanctuary where thoughts flowed effortlessly, where my soul whispered its secrets without hesitation. Each word bore the unmistakable essence of "Pandey," carrying my identity, my pain, my triumphs, and my fleeting joys. But now, as I stare at the pages, there's a bitterness that taints every letter. My writings, once companions in my solitude, now feel alien, detached, no longer mine.*

*It's as if they've betrayed me, deserting their creator to serve another master. The bond we shared has eroded, replaced by a disquieting sense of hate.*

*Not the fiery, explosive kind, but a slow-burning resentment. How could something I nurtured and cherished turn into a stranger, mocking my attempts to connect? I read my own words and feel nothing—not pride, not catharsis, not even recognition. They seem devoid of the essence that once made them "Pandey's."*

*The loss gnaws at me, relentless and unforgiving.*
*My writings were not just expressions; they were extensions of myself.*
*They held my voice, raw and unfiltered. But now, they feel like hollow imitations, void of the authenticity that once defined them.*
*I try to reclaim them, to pour myself into their veins again, but they resist, as if rejecting me. It's a heartbreak like no other—to lose something so deeply intertwined with one's being.*
*Perhaps it's my fault. Perhaps I've changed too much, or perhaps I've failed to keep up with my own evolution. My writings no longer reflect who I am—or worse, they reflect someone I don't recognize.*
*It's like looking into a mirror that distorts my image, showing a version of myself I cannot accept.*
*I want to scream, to demand answers, to know why this rift has formed. But the silence of the page offers no solace, only a cold indifference that deepens the void.*
*Hate, I realize, is a mask for the pain. Beneath the resentment lies a profound sense of loss—of identity, of purpose, of belonging. Writing was my anchor, grounding me when the world spun too fast. Without it, I feel unmoored, adrift in a sea of uncertainty.*
*I long for the days when my pen moved with conviction, when every word felt like a piece of my soul carved into permanence.*
*The pages now carry a weight they never did before—a suffocating heaviness that mirrors my own turmoil. Each attempt to write feels like a battle, not against the world but against myself.*
*My thoughts rebel, refusing to translate into words. The pen, once an extension of my hand, now feels foreign, as if it resents my touch.*
*And yet, I cannot let go. Despite the hate, despite the loss, there is a stubborn hope that clings to the edges of my despair.*
*Maybe, just maybe, I can mend this fractured bond.*
*Perhaps the essence of "Pandey" still lingers somewhere, buried beneath layers of doubt and disconnection.*

*I hold onto the faint hope that one day, my writings will feel like mine again—that they will once more be a reflection of my soul, unfiltered and true.*

*Until then, I wrestle with the estrangement, with the hate that masks my sorrow and the loss that haunts me. I write, not because it brings me joy but because it is the only way I know to fight back against the emptiness.*

*Each word, no matter how foreign, is a step toward reconciliation, a bridge to the connection I so desperately seek. In this struggle, I realize that hate and loss are not endpoints but part of the journey.*

*They are the shadows that make the light more precious, the silence that sharpens the longing for song. And so, I continue, pen in hand, chasing the fragments of myself that I once found so effortlessly in my words. For even in their estrangement, they remain a part of me—however distant, however changed.*

*And perhaps that is enough for now.*

*-Hritik.Y.Pandey*